BETTER THAN HEX

VIVIENNE SAVAGE

TABLE OF CONTENTS

CHAPTER 1

Thunder growled outside and shook the dilapidated mansion as lightning flashed beyond the dust-smeared windows. Debbie tiptoed through the musty corridors with a hammer clutched in her fist.

Would a hammer help against a ghost?

It couldn't be a ghost. Specters from the beyond didn't make footsteps.

A man of flesh and blood had to be lurking behind one of the doors in the creaking estate, and there was only one way to find out. With the police en route, she had less than five minutes until the murderer found her first, or they arrived to whisk her to safety.

A wooden board groaned behind her and she whirled, coming face to face with the knife-wielding murderer. It came whistling through the air and plunged into her shoulder, only to withdraw and slide forward again. It glided past her arm and sliced through flesh and tissue.

River Jackson, the sole spectator of the scary movie, shrieked and spilled her bowl of mixed popcorn and Sour Patch Kids gummies onto her lap. Melted butter stained her leggings, and specks of sugar glittered against them. She swore and placed the bowl on the empty couch cushion beside her.

Usually she ignored the jump scares, but the ambience of a dark room had taken its toll. She'd picked up the movie from a rental kiosk earlier that day, intending to watch it with her boyfriend once he dragged himself home from work.

But Zacarias was working late to meet an important deadline, and he'd called to tell her not to expect him until after nine. A glance at the clock showed it was closer to eleven.

"Stupid movie. It isn't even scary," River muttered under her breath. She'd already figured out the identity of the killer too, positive it was the heroine's boyfriend.

On the screen, Debbie fled into another room and shut the door on her assailant's arm, slamming her weight into it until the knife dropped from his fingers.

River paused the movie with the remote. She dealt often enough with supernatural boogeymen and monsters that horror movies with normal human beings shouldn't have had any effect on her.

A tap on the window dragged her gaze away from the flat-screen. She stared through narrowed eyes but saw nothing on the lit porch.

"Just a June bug or something. One of those big moths."

And now she was talking to herself like the heroine of some horror movie. Swallowing self-disgust, she wiped her hands on a napkin and reached for the remote.

Another creak reached her ears from the kitchen. The hairs on her nape rose.

"If someone's in there, I have a gun and a very large boyfriend."

Silence met her challenge. Only the first part of her threat was a lie though, but she couldn't exactly go around saying she was going to disintegrate someone with a hellacious ball of energy either.

"I'm losing it." Too much wine, an overdose of popcorn and sugar, and scary movies in the dark had made her paranoid.

After taking in a deep breath, she got up and moved toward the kitchen to fetch a glass of water. She'd need to remain hydrated to fend off a hangover in the morning, unless she wanted to brew a remedy in her cauldron.

Thanks to demolishing the wall dividing the halves of their duplex, River enjoyed a double-sized kitchen. They had adjoined the deck space, but Zacarias hadn't yet removed the additional sliding glass door leading to the veranda.

The additional door she'd closed and locked stood open to reveal a black rectangle of unlit rear yard. Hot, muggy air wafted inside, and the distinct hum of a mosquito buzzed in her ears.

Someone was in her house.

Too fast for River's human eyes to follow, a dark blur shot across the room. She threw out her hands and molded her willpower into a single incantation. The wave of heat rushed at her attacker, condensed into a sphere of orange and red flames.

It struck the target and broke apart on impact, sending embers and small bits of burning spell matter drifting to the ground like snowflakes. A high-pitched yowl reverberated through the house and transformed into distinctive swears in a familiar voice.

"Zac?" Her heartbeat spiked even further, until the racing pulse pounded behind her eyes.

"Yeah, *querida*. It's me."

Darling? He had the nerve to "darling" her after nearly making her pee in the kitchen? Between her wine bladder and his immature prank, her temper flared to nuclear range.

"What the hell?" River demanded. "I could have killed you!"

"But you didn't," Zacarias replied, although smoke and the smell of singed fur still wafted off his human body— his naked human body. Despite some of the paranormal romance books she read, she'd yet to meet a real shapeshifter capable of transforming with his clothes. Not that she minded. It made for interesting social times.

Needing a moment to recover from her ordeal, she leaned against the wall with a palm pressed against her heaving chest. Her life had flashed before her eyes, and the only thing protecting Zac from her wrath was the fact that half of those visions included him.

"You're such a... a..."

"Lovable asshole too sexy for you to resist?" Zacarias's Brazilian accent rolled off the tongue like auditory sex. And as much as River loved to hear it, he couldn't have chosen a worse time to play one of his practical jokes.

"An asshole who gets to sleep on the couch, that's what."

"Aw, River, come on. Don't be that way."

"You should have thought better about scaring me. You told me you'd be home by nine."

He sighed. "I said I'd be home *after* nine. We had a large business deal to complete with a Japanese software company. Time zone difference."

She crossed her arms over her chest and glowered while Zac put on his best pout, like two hundred pounds of Puss 'n' Boots.

"I heard a noise outside on the porch."

"That was me. I saw the text you sent about the movie being lame, and when I noticed you were too zoned out to see me outside, I thought I'd have some fun." He quieted and folded his arms. "I'm sorry, all right? I won't do it again. You used to like playing gags on each other."

"Yeah, *harmless* gags. I could have hurt you, and I would have felt awful about it."

"I'm sorry, Riv, really."

She drew in a deep breath through her nose and nodded. Zac stepped over and pulled her to him, hugging her against his chest with his cheek on her head. She wrapped her arms around his waist and closed her eyes.

"I guess you can sleep in the bed," she muttered. "The couch is a mess anyway."

Zacarias smiled. "I saw that."

She vacuumed up popcorn and wiped a few spots of butter off the microfiber couch with a damp, sudsy washcloth while Zac gathered his clothes from outside. He joined her in his boxers, clothes folded over one arm.

"Hey," River said as she peered out the window. "Where's your car?"

"Caught a flat on I-35 and my ride doesn't carry a spare. Harrison gave me a ride home once we towed the Jag down to Pete's Autobody."

"Why didn't you call me? I would have come to get you."

"Wasn't sure if you'd be awake, and Harrison was closer. He takes the same highway home, remember?"

"Oh. Yeah." Her heart fluttered with disappointment. He could have called. Ten seconds to text her a warning.

He canted his head. "You okay?"

"Yeah, fine." She forced a smile and shook her insecurities away. "I think I'm gonna go to bed."

"Already? I just came home. We can finish your movie."

"I think I'm horror-movied out for the night." She lifted to her toes and kissed his cheek before moving toward the hall. "Night," she called over a shoulder to him.

"Night, Riv."

As much as she loved her panther, he knew how to push her buttons and provoke her to violence. It may have felt like they'd lived together for years, but they'd only begun renovating the inside of their duplex and knocking down walls two months ago.

Her father thought she was crazy for the decision, but her mother thought darling Zacarias was sweeter than apple pie and the ideal catch of a lifetime.

As always, her divorced parents could never make up their minds and took contrary stances on every subject related to their daughter's life.

Combining her home with Zacarias's place might not have been the wisest decision, but it had been the choice her heart wanted to make. And she didn't regret it. They now had twice the space, love, laughter, and happiness. He cooked, and she did laundry. He mowed the lawn, and she tended the garden. Despite his offer to foot all expenses, River had been happy to divide their bills down the middle. Having a rich boyfriend didn't mean she had to live off him and lose her independence.

"I really am sorry for scaring you," Zacarias said again. A glance over her shoulder revealed his contrite expression, like she'd not only kicked his puppy but drowned a sack of his kittens along with it. As he sulked, his black hair flopped onto his forehead. He always waited weeks past needing a haircut.

"Oh geez. Fine. You make some snacks, and I'll start this movie over."

After all, who could stay mad at the world's most perfect guy for long?

***

River toiled above a steaming cauldron while her fascinated boyfriend observed from behind her. He didn't often spectate her brewing rituals. The simmering mixture bubbled and popped, thin tendrils of lavender smoke wafting up from the surface. She stirred with a glass rod, turning it left and right in alternating patterns.

"This is kind of morbid. Why so many body parts?" he asked, as she plucked a single newt eye from a jar she kept in the mini-fridge nearby.

"Because every object in this world has its own magical value. Even you," she explained with the patience of a saint. *Whole package,* she reminded herself. She had to love the whole package. Good looks, chiseled abs, and innate shapeshifter curiosity. She smiled up at him despite his hovering.

"You poured that in blind but added drops of that. What's the difference?" As inquisitive as a cat, he leaned until he invaded her space, practically putting his chin on her shoulder. He couldn't help it, and she wouldn't have him any other way. Except for when she was brewing dangerously volatile potions that could blow up their home.

"Because one drop too many of this reagent will cause the whole potion to explode on us," she explained.

Zac backed away. "Ah. Right. Hands off."

River chuckled and counted out the last three drops. The mixture shimmered and went from warm, cocoa brown to indigo, while she leaned forward over it. After the aroma of sage and the metallic bite of iron invaded her nose, she glanced across the room at the tiny Snellen Vision Test chart she'd printed out that morning.

Flawless vision at twice the intended viewing distance. The lowest line read with the same clarity as the top, and she'd barely breathed more than a whiff.

Pleased, she straightened and screwed the dropper into the bottle again. The scent of garden herbs, Zac's soap, and her own shampoo wafted around her along with the meadow-fresh scent of fabric softener.

A perfect enhancement of her olfactory senses too.

"There we go, all done. You can rub my shoulders to your heart's content while it cools."

Zacarias stepped closer again and wrapped his arm around her middle. Arms like bands of steel secured her in place against him. "I have intentions to do more than rub your shoulders now that you've forgiven me."

She couldn't stay mad, and the light of day had brought humor to the previous night's misadventure. Somewhat.

"Promises, promises," she said.

Zac grinned then nodded toward the cauldron. "What does that do anyway?"

"It's a keen senses potion, used most often by witches preferring not to rely on your kind during investigations. Not that it really compares with the nose of a really experienced shapeshifter. But it's good enough."

"They're all merely jealous they don't have a panther at their beck and call. Anyway, what would happen if *I* took that potion?"

"You'd be miserable for hours."

"What? Not super-panther?"

"More like super-overloaded panther."

River imagined finding him in the closet, hiding in the dark and burying his nose in the piles of unused winter blankets.

"So, perhaps my biggest question is this: if you are not the one using it, why do you brew it?"

"Because I'm the coven brewmaster and this was requisitioned."

Of course, the title was brand-new and she hadn't yet shared it with him because Zacarias thought she already put immense amounts of time into what could be thankless work for the witch's council. With her teeth edging her lower lip, she stole a glance at him and held her breath.

The strong arms dropped away when Zacarias stepped back to look at her. "Coven brewmaster? When did they give you *more* work?"

River ran her bare toes over the floor and avoided eye contact. "A month ago. Georgina has her hands full with tutoring witches who want to learn, so she can't be our main supplier too."

"Why am I just finding out about this? Were you not saying they had already stressed you enough?"

"This is a promotion, Zac. Besides, everyone in the coven has to contribute in some way."

"Right, right, unless you are a lone witch."

She nodded. "Right. We witches keep to our circles for a reason, and being alone is the path to darkness."

"You're not a Jedi."

She pressed her lips together and crossed her arms over her chest. "Remember your ex? The lone witch?"

Zacarias stiffened. They hadn't discussed his ex-wife often in the nine months since she'd tried brewing lust potions to take control of him. His entire expression changed, turning guarded and closed. "She'd have gone bad whether she had people around her or not. You aren't good because of the coven, River. You're good because you're you. A good person with a good heart."

His faith in her was humbling.

"I'm sorry I didn't tell you about the new position sooner," she apologized, voice quiet. "This is going to be good for me, Zac. Good for us. It means I have their trust and access to more of the coven resources. Books, equipment, components... you name it."

"None of that explains why more work is good for *us*."

His grumble made her smile, and she leaned up, kissing his jaw. "This won't be as much as you think. I'm not going to be chained to my potions table or anything. Besides, I'm only brewing these for the witch assigned to handle the real work," she assured him.

"Fine." He paused, then added, "What work?"

His insatiable curiosity never failed to amuse her.

"You know, I didn't think to even ask."

His warm breath huffed across her throat as he turned his face into her neck. "I miss having more of your time without scheduling in advance. It's like I need to make an appointment to be with my own girlfriend now."

"Then let's have unscheduled fun tonight."

"Sounds good. What did you have in mind?"

"It's not very fun or unscheduled if we plan it out," she teased.

Zac nipped her ear. "Fine. You shower while I make dinner."

"Are you trying to say I stink?"

He leaned in and sniffed her. "No, not stink, but you do smell like guts and stuff. Not exactly conducive to a romantic evening on the couch. I'm not *that* kind of shifter."

She pushed him off. "All right, Romeo, you win. I'll go get cleaned up and slip into something a little more comfortable."

CHAPTER 2

Zacarias had the perfect setting for a romantic night. They'd eat dinner, have wine, and then he'd coax her up to their bedroom for a night under the silky brand-new sheets. With a grin on his face, he dimmed the living room lights.

He glanced at River, taking in the sight of her in only a thin halter top and cut-off shorts that covered no more than her favorite pair of full-coverage panties. She only wore the shorts in the house for him, never outside, and he was fine with that. Although he didn't consider himself possessive, he struggled to suppress some shifter instincts on a day-to-day basis. And keeping guys off River was one of them. The beast inside him demanded respect.

When Zac made another trip to the kitchen to fetch the wine and both glasses, he paused by the phone and checked the caller ID. His mother's Brazilian phone number popped up as one of the recent calls.

"Mom called today. Did you talk to her?" he called into the living room.

"Oh, yeah. Sorry, it completely slipped my mind." River finished lighting some candles and glanced over her shoulder.

"What'd she want?"

"To make sure we were still planning to visit later this summer."

Zac sucked in a quiet breath and studied her from the archway, a frosty bottle of apricot wine held in his left hand. "What did you tell her?"

"That we were going to look at plane tickets this week, as promised," she replied. "That's what we agreed on, right?"

"Yeah, yeah. You're still cool with going, right?"

"Of course I wanna go." River laughed and patted the spot beside her on the sofa. "I can't wait to meet your mom in person."

The tightness in his chest released in an instant, returning the grin to his face as he crossed the room to join her. "Good, I'm glad. We won't even have to fight our way onto the crowded beaches. You're going to love her pool."

He hoped she would love more than the pool. His mom was eager to meet her and even more anxious to hand down his grandmother's engagement ring. All he had left to do was pop the question, but he wanted the moment to be perfect.

Their plans moved flawlessly after dinner until a massive SUV roared into the driveway. River twisted around and peered out the window.

"Hey, why are the guys outside?" she asked.

The driver laid on the horn when Zacarias didn't emerge, like they had plans or…

"Shit." He held his glass in one hand and the remote to their PlayStation 4 in the other. Netflix and chill had been his intentions since he'd lured her out of the brewing room.

The passenger door opened and his friend, Harrison, hopped out.

"Shit what? What's going on?" River asked.

He sank down on the couch. "Quick, let's pretend we aren't home and sneak upstairs."

"Too late, he waved at me through the window," she said.

Zacarias set the bottle on the coffee table and met their wereraven friend at the door. It didn't take much of an imagination to see the similarities between him and his animal form. His wiry frame, intelligent eyes, and glossy blue-black hair made him resemble his corvid cousins.

Harrison had his hand raised to knock but dropped it to his side and grinned. "Come on, man. We're waiting on you."

River squeezed into the doorframe beside him. "Hi, Harrison. I hate to break it to you, but if you had plans with Mr. CRS, he forgot them… but I may be willing to relinquish my claim for the night depending on where you're going." She flashed him a sweet smile and made a gesture with her fingers to indicate her eyes were "up here" when Harrison's attention drifted down to her legs instead.

To make the reminder stick, Zac jabbed him in the shoulder. "CRS?"

"Ow! Uh. The Sin Den. And she's right, you can't remember shit."

The smile dropped off her face. "Seriously?"

"Yeah. We planned this two weeks ago," Harrison said, puffing up like a bird on a wire. "They're running their Fourth of July specials all month. It's very patriotic."

"Strippers," River repeated. Zac saw the gears moving in her head. She was weighing the options, deciding whether or not their relationship could be damaged by an innocent night of ogling breasts.

Harrison rubbed his shoulder and said defensively, "The drinks are great."

Zac chuckled. "I can stay home."

"Dude, you promised. Didn't you bow out last time?"

"Yeah, I did but—"

"He's going with you guys. As much as I'd love to keep him home, I'm not going to be that girl. Enjoy some time with your friends, Zac. I'll be right here when you get back."

"You sure after the shit I just gave you a couple hours ago?"

"Yeah. Besides, this is different, and I know if our situations were reversed and I'd forgotten a social engagement with the witches, you'd send me along too." Her bright eyes drifted to the vehicle full of rowdy guys waving to her from the drive. She waved back.

"You're the best, girl," Darrell called out the rear passenger-side window. The other men quickly agreed and cheered her.

"I still can't believe you're taking my man away to a freaking peep show," River complained with an exaggerated huff. A smile crept onto her face. "Patriotic, my ass."

His girlfriend was five and a half feet of curvy perfection. Everything from her painted toes up to her head of glossy brown ringlets was all his, and he couldn't imagine ever wanting anyone else. And soon, once he worked up the courage, she'd be more than a girlfriend, promoted from live-in-lady to future wife since he'd already given her that title in his heart.

"It's not a peep show," Harrison said in an exasperated tone.

"Oh yeah?" River challenged him.

"It's called a strip club, and you know, if you want, you can come along to hang with us. I mean, it's cool if you do. Tommy's wife comes out sometimes," Harrison said.

"No," she squeaked out, staring at them with wide eyes. She flapped her hands around and stepped back from the door. "I do not want to come along to watch him stuff dollars in some thang's G-string, thank you very much."

Zacarias grinned even wider. "Don't gotta go if it bothers you, you know. I'll stay home."

"As you've said for the second or third time. No," she said, shaking her head. "I trust you. I just think it's gross, but I want you to spend time with them. Just... don't let some chick shove her cooch in your face, okay?"

"Your cooch is the only one I want in my face," he told her honestly.

"You're both ridiculous," Harrison groaned. "It's only one night out, man, and you act like we're kidnapping you at gunpoint."

River rolled her eyes. "Go. Have fun," she said as she pushed him out the door and onto the porch. "Abduct him, but bring him back in one piece."

"Awesome. Promise to return him safe and sound."

She stood on tiptoe, kissed her boyfriend goodbye, and disappeared into the living room.

Damn. Zacarias would have gladly overruled her decree and stayed with her if he hadn't already canceled plans twice in the past. She was right to send him, he knew that, but it didn't change how much he would have preferred getting drunk and laid now as opposed to later once they returned him home.

Harrison practically stuffed him into the Tahoe waiting in the drive. A chorus of voices greeted Zac, all of them male this time, despite Harrison's earlier comment. Sometimes Ceres *did* join them for a night out, and sometimes she drank the boys all under the table. Werewolf bitches were like that, and the guys quickly grew to love when she accompanied them.

It kinda made Zacarias wish River would cut loose the same way, but she'd probably combust and melt into an embarrassed puddle if he bought her a lap dance. He liked to tease her about it though, because she designed sultry romance book covers for a living. She could photoshop bare-chested men holding women in lingerie all day long, but strip dances flustered her.

"You have no idea how glad I am that you're the one driving tonight, man," Zac said.

Tommy glanced back from the driver's seat and grinned. "You're not the only one who thinks the interior of Bobby's van smells like a pile of old gym socks. Em let me borrow her ride for the night." His single cab truck wouldn't hold all their friends, and Zac's Jag certainly wouldn't.

"Em's sweet," Zac replied.

Emma was Tommy's second wife. He had two, or rather, the three of them shared each other equally in a polyamorous shifter bond.

"How do you borrow something you paid for?" Bobby grumbled.

"Actually, she makes all the payments now. Her bakery is taking off."

"Not fair. You shifters claim all the hot ladies with jobs who don't want sugar daddies," Bobby said. "How's a normal guy supposed to get laid when you dudes take everything? Two of everything sometimes, like this greedy jerk."

Tommy snickered at Bobby's halfhearted complaint. "You know, I'd turn you if you wanted," he offered. "Or let Ceres do it, if you prefer a woman putting her teeth on you. I think it gets her all hot and bothered when she gets to pop a human's werecherry." Wolves were one of the few shifter breeds able to transfer their magical powers through a bite.

"Thought about it last time you said that. It's a long, one-way road to travel," Bobby said. "Not that it wouldn't be nice to add a few more decades on my life and maintain this kind of sex appeal, but—"

Laughter erupted from the rear seat first then spread throughout the SUV. Bobby was a great guy, and so were their other two human pals, Darrell and Patrick. But none of them had taken Tommy up on the offer to join the wild side, because they were satisfied with their lives or scared of the outcome.

"What? I'm sexy."

"You sure are," Tommy said, snickering.

"Speaking of sexy, get a load of Darrell's biceps. The jerk finally beat me at arm wrestling," Patrick grumbled.

Zac twisted around and looked at his two pals. "Got some guns working that new construction project? I thought you hated working out."

"No, I hate hitting the gym with you unnatural freaks," Darrell shot back, a big grin on his face. "This is a paying job, and if I get ripped in the process, all the better."

"Hey, man, I heard y'all lost another worker. You sure the pay is worth that risk?" Bobby asked.

"That guy was an idiot who messed with the wiring without his gloves on," Darrell said. "If you're smart, follow the rules, and keep your head in the game, you're fine. I mean, I'm sorry the guy died—"

"He's like the, what, third one now?" Tommy asked from the front.

"Ah, man, I'm not counting, and this is depressing talk for our night out," Darrell protested.

In under an hour, they reached their destination outside of Austin's city limits. A tilted spotlight lit up the sky beside a scarlet building identified by a neon sign as the Sin Den. Zac snickered every time he saw it.

After passing a distracted, glassy-eyed bouncer, they paid the cover fee and found a table inside. The place was quiet for a weekend night, but he chalked it up to the recent movie release in the theaters.

"Guy looked like he was on something," Bobby muttered.

"Yeah, he did," Darrell said. "Kinda unprofessional, but what can you do?"

Tommy settled back with a thoughtful expression on his face, which ended once Patrick arrived with pitchers of beer from the bar. His nose remained wrinkled.

"What's up with you?" Zac asked, nudging him.

"Smelled something rank," Tommy muttered. "Don't worry about it."

Before Zac could press him, a pair of dancers arrived in lace-trimmed bras and panties. The first girl was caramel brown with wild curls surrounding her heart-shaped face, reminding him of River without the dynamic curves, round behind, and jiggle to her thighs. Her companion fit the description of Snow White—skin as fair as fresh cream, rosy cheeks, scarlet lips, and dark hair. Harrison zeroed in on her and sat ramrod straight in his seat. Zac grinned.

Money practically exploded from Harrison's wallet once "Lily" introduced herself, and then it became a mad race for the gang to outdo him. Zacarias lost count of the dirty looks Harrison shot the rest of them each time they lured Lily away from him with more cash.

It was for his own good. The dancers weren't looking for love.

The first hour passed with strong drinks, idle conversation, and familiar club music. Patrick left the table to sit by the stage, eager to see his favorite entertainer's nightly performance. There was a girl who danced like a wild cat spliced with a firecracker, and tonight she looked the part in her sequined red, white, and blue boy shorts. She moved up and down the pole as if she'd been born on it, twisting and performing acrobatics an Olympic judge could respect.

"We need to do this more often. Once a month ain't enough," Bobby said.

Recently, the gang had been too busy with their individual lives to catch up and hang out. Between the renovations at Zacarias's house and Harrison hounding him to pick up his end of the work in their partnership, Zacarias barely had a moment to breathe because he was always chasing down River to find time with her. Tommy had a busy home life keeping two wives and an adopted son happy. Patrick had an up-and-coming rock band, Bobby was working on his doctorate, and Darrell worked construction for his uncle during the summer—right now, they had an enormous gig outside of Atropos building a new subdivision full of expensive homes in the low-to-middle six-digit range.

"I'm so glad we started coming here instead of that shit hole in San Antonio," Bobby said as a bare-breasted redhead slid her fingers down his shoulders and then guided both of his hands over her thighs. Her glittery pasties were as rosy as the nipples beneath.

"Freaking three-foot rule," Darrell muttered in agreement. "Whoever heard of strip clubs where you can't get a lap dance?"

Zac shook his head. River would bounce up and down on his lap as much as he wanted once he was home, but for the moment, he feigned interest in helping some girl pay her college tuition. To justify wasting the money, he made up scenarios in his head, creating reasons for why the entertainers jiggled their boobs in front of them.

Then he caught a whiff of something sweet with a metallic bite—something sweeter than honey, like fresh flowers on a summer day, masking something more nefarious. Darker.

The smell of copper and blood clung to "Lily's" skin and wafted from her hair each time her nubile body moved. Then it became a sumptuous aroma, delicate and fragrant, like honeysuckle and a crisp, white wine.

She undulated and rolled her hips, bending her knees as she dropped her tight ass to the floor. The pale-skinned, brunette stripper was as nimble as a ballet dancer, magnificent to behold.

A sensation of arousal crept over Zacarias's otherwise disinterested body, something he'd experienced before when his ex-wife, a dark witch, tried to use sex-magic to lure him back to her.

Someone had cast a spell on him.

That was the thing about mind-altering spells. Once they were cast and a person was aware of how it felt, they'd never forget the experience.

Sudden clarity struck. "Lily" was pale for all the wrong reasons, because the intoxicating scent coming from her wasn't perfume. The stripper was a vampire. At that moment, her magical hooks vanished and Zac tore free from the enchantment.

He glanced to the left to see Tommy sitting stiffly in his chair, his spine rigid and his jaw clenched as the redhead ran her fingers through his hair. Zac and Tommy's gazes met briefly. The wolf must have noticed it too.

A quick glance to the right indicated their friends had been mesmerized. Harrison and Patrick forked over money in a daze, unaware of their surroundings. The most disturbing realization came as Zacarias noticed the six of them were alone in the club.

Where had the rest of the customers gone? When had they been hustled out of the strip club? The bartender stood behind the counter with a vacant expression on her face, swaying to the music and unaware of her surroundings.

She was in thrall, as were a few of the other dancers, making it easy to pick out vamp from human without having to rely on his nose. The ginger was either a vampire pet or an innocent bystander, but they had to err on the side of caution and believe she was capable of anything.

Tommy stood up first. "I'm only asking once. Let our friends out of your trance now."

"Lily" twirled around the pole a final time before coming to a stop, so still she may as well have been a statue. "Now, why would I want to do that? Look how happy they are."

Zacarias scooted back from the small table and rose from his seat. "I'd listen to him."

"Trance?" Harrison came out of it on his own, appearing bewildered. "What trance? What's going on?" He glanced around. "And why's it so empty?"

"You were salivating over a vampire," Zac informed him.

Elongated fangs gleamed in the dim lighting when a second vampire stepped on the stage, hissed, and narrowed her red eyes. "Can't a girl enjoy a meal?" She licked the pole slowly, the gesture filled with innuendo.

She was toying with them, trying to keep their attention on her pretty face instead of the assault creeping up from the rear. Zac heard the distinct scrape of boots from behind them. Two more vampires, by the smell of them.

In a few swift movements, he unfastened his belt, flicked open the button on his jeans, and dove forward from two human legs onto four panther's paws. The T-shirt ripped around his furry, bulkier torso.

What the movies didn't tell people was that it took a lot of strength to shove a blunt object into a vampire's chest through the protective sternum connecting both halves of the ribs. Hunters couldn't accomplish it without training.

So most shifters didn't bother with the stake-to-the-heart crap. They ripped them apart first. A vamp could only heal so much damage before they lost all their vital fluid, and after that, they were sitting ducks and vulnerable to anything.

Tommy, suddenly a wall of muscle covered in dark fur, bounded past Zacarias's left side. While he went for the girl, Zac whirled to go after the two behind them. As a panther, he had the bigger teeth and more intimidating claws.

A male vampire crossed the distance from the bar to the table in one lunge, his mouth yawning open and his claws out. Roaring, Zac dove at him. They clashed like two lions in the savannah, snarling and snapping.

The second vampire, a small, fragile female bloodsucker, jumped onto his back and buried her fangs into his shoulder. Harrison sprang to his timely rescue and slammed a chair into her. As she was dislodged from her perch, pain ripped down Zac's shoulder.

Then the thralls joined the fray. A half dozen screaming maniacs rushed in with whatever weapons they could find, from chairs to beer bottles and serving trays.

"Hurry and kill the leeches," Harrison shouted. "Kill them before their thralls kill us."

Moving by feral instinct and driven nearly mad with the pain from the bite, the panther knocked his opponent's arm aside and seized him by the face. The smell of a new youngblood clung to the vampire's flesh, marking him as a weak neophyte too fresh to have learned how to use his supernatural prowess. The vamp writhed and screamed out, his strikes glancing off the shifter's hard body until his skull cracked into powder and a pile of brittle bones formed beneath Zacarias.

From the stage area, Zac heard visceral ripping followed by a shriek. "Lily" raced past them for the exit, only for Tommy to tackle her from behind. On the stage, he saw blood and more bones. Tommy had killed Patrick's favorite dancer.

No wonder she had sweet moves. And judging from the way Lily evaded Tommy, she could have been the other girl's teacher. She moved like she was boneless, rolling and flipping, maneuvering around Tommy, while always staying one step ahead of his jaws. Finally, he caught her by the calf and slammed her against the ground.

"Zac, kill her," Harrison yelled. He held up a chair in the nick of time. One of the ensorcelled human strippers bashed a bottle against the back of it, shattering the glass and splashing alcohol everywhere.

The mournful loss of good booze upset Zacarias as much as the attack.

As a couple others closed in to surround them, Zac leapt up from the pile of ashes and lunged for his quarry. When his claws sank into her back, he knew she didn't have a chance in hell of escaping. He made short work of her, decapitating her with one ferocious bite to her throat.

Once they cut the metaphorical strings to the vampires' marionettes, the thralls collapsed and fell to the floor. None of them moved, aside from the subtle rise and fall of their chests.

"Is it safe now?" Bobby asked from somewhere in the room.

Zacarias followed the sound of Bobby's voice to the exit, where he saw a trio of coat stands, then he sniffed the air. A strained and exhausted Harrison let the illusion drop. In place of the coat stands, their three human friends stared with expressions ranging from terror to admiration.

"Holy shit. Those were vampires," Bobby blurted out. "You killed vampires in front of us."

"Bad ass," Patrick said. "Epic battle between werewolf and a vampire witnessed. I can scratch that off my bucket list."

"Dude, you aren't freaked out?" Bobby demanded.

"Hell no. It was like the ultimate 3-D experience to our favorite movies. I'm sure once the adrenaline fades, I'll be pissing myself, but right now... *awesome.*"

Darrell remained silent. He sagged against the wall and stared with wide, unseeing eyes, his ashen face and motionless posture worrying Zac the most.

"I can't believe they didn't see us," Bobby said. "Fuck, I can't believe we're *alive.* We survived that. We survived a vampire attack."

"Never had to veil so many people at once," Harrison admitted. Raven shifters had a reputation for making mischief with their illusion magic. "Normally, I'd—oh shit, Tommy's covered in blood."

"I'll be fine. You guys all right?" Tommy asked. He ignored that he was leaking blood all over the floor and stepped into his jeans. Zac did the same. Their human pals weren't weirded out by random nudity anymore, but he still didn't want to stand around with his piece out.

"My head's a little fuzzy, but yeah," Patrick replied. "I'm more worried about you guys. Both of you are bleeding."

Zac glanced at his back in one of the mirrored walls. The wound was already closing, unlike the nasty diagonal slash across Tommy's chest.

Considering the circumstances, he didn't think anyone would mind if he helped himself to the bar. He poured shots of whiskey for everyone and shoved a glass into Darrell's hand. He was shaking the most.

Harrison groaned into both palms and paced into a small circle. "Okay. There's security footage rolling right now. Let's wipe that and any evidence that we were here. Tommy, you trash the vamp remains. The thralls should come around again soon, and we need to be gone before they're awake."

Taking charge came naturally for Harrison, since his family handled everything from occult coverups to magical espionage. The work had been bred into his blood. Years of cleaning up after werewolves had honed the raven clan's skills when it came to hiding supernatural activity. It was their calling, their favorite job above all other tasks, and they were hired by all the heavy hitters across the world to clean up the messes other paranormal creatures made.

"Do you think the vamps would have allowed cameras to record their activities?" Tommy asked.

"They were dumb enough to try feeding from a werejaguar and werewolf," Harrison shot back.

Half an hour later, not only had Harrison found the security cameras recording a digital feed, but he'd also deleted it, verified it hadn't been transmitted over the Internet, and scrubbed all evidence of it while making it appear to be a technical error.

"This isn't normal," Harrison said. "They should have realized three of us are shifters, that we're off limits. Tommy is an alpha, my dad leads our unkindness—"

"Worst name ever for a group of crows," Bobby cut in. "Your people are as kind as it gets."

Harrison grunted. "Ravens, not crows. Anyway, me and him are doubly off limits. They should have realized you or Tommy would sniff them out."

"Did you notice they were vamps before the attack?" Zac asked.

Harrison shook his head. "I don't have your nose. You should have said something when you saw the others in a trance, kitty."

Zac ignored him and stomped on the weakened bones left by the vampire killed in the doorway. They crumbled to ash with minimal effort. "I only realized a minute before they attacked. Besides, seeing a vampire isn't always cause for alarm. All of them aren't killers."

"Most of them are," Harrison challenged.

"Anyway, I realized a few seconds later that they weren't up to any good, and by then, Tommy was on to it too."

"So what's the difference between a trance and a thrall?" Patrick asked.

"A vampire can put a weak-minded human into a temporary trance. They're not a thrall until they've had, well, I don't actually know how much blood it takes," Zac admitted. "Thralls are bound to their vampire patron. After that, they're stronger and faster than the average human and their willpower can be stolen from them without notice."

"Weak-minded?" Bobby blurted out.

"Shut it, guys. I'm calling Argus to report this," Tommy growled. He had a phone raised to his ear. In situations like this, whenever he spoke to his father-in-law about business matters concerning their packs, he transitioned from fun-loving pal to stern-faced werewolf leader.

After a few seconds of terse silence, the wolf grunted into the phone. "All right. Talk to you at the estate," he said before hanging up. "Argus says it's unusual for vampires to attack shifters unprovoked. If they're travelers or rogues apart from a bigger coven, their leader should have notified all shifter alphas of their arrival to the city."

"And if they're not travelers?" Patrick asked curiously.

"Then they belong to the local vampire house and they're gonna answer for this."

"Did Captain Obvious have anything else to say on the matter?" Harrison asked.

Tommy nodded. "Yeah. He said it's also possible they were lone vamps, young and unaware of all the rules. If no one taught them to announce their arrival to the shifters, they couldn't know."

"Nobody carries around silver weapons in this day and age, so they must have known you were coming, dude." Zac gestured to his friend's chest. Blood continued to seep from his wound, filling the air with a horrible, acidic odor.

Injure a werewolf badly enough with silver, and he'd bleed to death in hours.

He grunted. "Agreed. Every vampire in the state knows San Antonio to Austin is territory to two wolf packs."

"So what you guys are saying is that some crazy vampire-stripper assassin just tried to off Tommy? See, this is why I'm not down with the full moon squad," Bobby said.

"Are you going to be okay, man?" Darrell finally spoke up.

"Yeah. It's minor. She only scraped me, so I should be fine."

The longer he stared at the oozing slash, the less certain Zacarias felt about its outlook. "Pretty serious for a scrape. I'll feel better about it if you come in and see River. She can slap some crap on that and send you home."

River had a cure for every ailment in that potion room of hers, and his conscience wouldn't let him send Tommy home without a check.

CHAPTER 3

When lights from a parking car flashed through River's living room windows, she leapt up from the couch and shuffled to the door. The peaceful night without Zac had passed with books long overdue for a read, wine-sipping, and casually catching up with old friends on Facebook.

Their early arrival was unexpected, however. A boys' night out tended to last until well after midnight.

She leaned out the door and raised one hand to shield her eyes from the bright headlights. Men began spilling out after the driver killed the engine.

"You guys back already? Who got sick enough to need a remedy?" The boys knew she could brew the basic home remedies for most ailments, and they'd utilized her talents in the past.

"It's not alcohol poisoning," Zac replied as he stepped from the driver's side door. Her man approached in ripped jeans, his T-shirt missing. The denim was filthy and covered in ash.

"Why do you all look like you've been through hell?"

"We *have* been," Bobby said.

Tommy stumbled forward, allowing her to see why Zac had driven them home. With blood running down his arm and across his chest, the pale alpha needed Patrick's help to stand.

"How long has he been bleeding like this?"

"A little more than a half hour. Wouldn't let us take him to a hospital," Bobby said.

"It wasn't so bad at first," Tommy mumbled. "Just a scratch."

"Clean him up so I can see what I'm dealing with. He's covered in blood." She'd never seen a werewolf bleed so much before. Usually even their serious wounds began closing on their own within a few minutes.

"Silver. This bloodsucking bitch carved him up with silver," Patrick blurted out. "He wasn't like this a half hour ago. He was hallucinating on the way here, talking to his grandma and shit, Riv."

Tommy's grandmother had died years ago. River froze, and as her heart slammed into a racing rhythm, she stepped forward to assess the depth of the cut. The flesh hadn't been laid open to the bone, but it required stitches, and River had no formal medical training. "He called this a scratch? We need to get Ceres—"

"No. Don't call her," Tommy insisted. "She'll rip me a new one, and Emma will rip me a third."

"Forget the shower. You guys get him into the guest room. Zac, you hold pressure on the wound while I grab my stuff. He needs stitches."

Months ago, when they first began to remodel their duplex and knock down the walls separating each half of the building, Zac had been the one to insist on River keeping her own space. One of the spare bedrooms became her brewing chamber, a place to stock potions, ingredients, and all the weird stuff he didn't want in the kitchen. A guy only had to find a bag of goat eyeballs in his refrigerator once before buying his girl her own mini-fridge.

Darrell had helped him install cabinets with marble countertops, sturdy shelves, and a real cast-iron wood-burning stove for her cauldron. Now, that same cauldron would save their friend's life.

She hurried to the recipe book propped open on the pedestal beside the mixing pot, but an idea clicked in her head before she had a chance to find the entry on werewolves.

After pulling on gloves, she opened a bottle of dried wolfbane from the shelf. It was a strong poison in itself, and she didn't want it on her hands. According to lore, it repelled werewolves from gardens and weakened their powers. A better, more practical use was to temporarily suppress his allergies to silver along with the rest of his gifts.

Like a woman possessed, she hurried from shelf to shelf gathering rare ingredients and common herbs. A pinch here, a spoonful there, a single thorn from a rose. She had never brewed a wolfbane potion in her life, but somehow the knowledge came to her by instinct—the recipe as natural as one she'd made a thousand times before.

As she crumbled the dried wolfbane leaves into steaming rainwater, Harrison called out from the guest room, "Hey, how's that potion coming along? I don't wanna rush you, but he's not looking good."

"I need fifteen minutes."

Quality took time, time made magic, magic saved lives. River repeated the mantra over and over in her head while the ingredients cooked.

Sweat beaded on her brow as she lit a bundle of dried lavender sprigs above the alchemical brew, waved its smoke, and chanted. She needed it for the healing properties.

Please, Tommy. Hold out and wait on me.

A single pinch of fairy dust glittered over the surface. She stirred with a golden rod until fragrant bubbles infused with the essence of lavender formed on the surface. An oil-slick sheen glistened seconds later, reflecting beautiful shades of gold, pink, and teal.

Without understanding why, she knew it was ready.

After pouring the concoction into a mug, she hurried into the guest room. The guys gathered around the bed with worried faces.

"You guys are lucky I expected hangovers and had the stove warmed already, or this would have taken much longer."

Patrick crouched beside the bed, holding a wet washcloth in one of his hands while Zac applied pressure to Tommy's wound. "I guess it's a good thing you watch out for us. What's that gonna do?"

"It'll render the silver harmless to him before he bleeds to death. But he has to drink all of it and it's gotta be right now."

They helped him sit up, and despite the steam rising from it, Tommy scalded his mouth to sip it. He grimaced but chugged the rest down.

"Now what?" Darrell asked.

"We wait. Despite what movies and games would have you believe, magic isn't instantaneous." River smoothed Tommy's hair back from his sweaty brow.

Anxiety rolled through River's stomach and twisted her confidence into knots. It could be an hour or more before they knew if Tommy was out of the woods, so she lingered to keep close tabs on him.

Had she made the right choice or worsened his predicament? What had she been thinking, following instincts instead of adhering to advice from the book?

Witches did it on occasion. After all, it was how they learned and discovered new recipes for their books, but there were better times to put her magical prowess to the test than experimenting on a close friend.

"He doesn't look any better yet," Zac said in a low voice.

She eyed the red hives dotting Tommy's skin. He was looking worse by the second, and the disconcerting croaking sound coming from his throat reminded River of her brush with anaphylaxis after a wasp encounter.

"Find some Benadryl for him, Zac, and grab my EpiPen from my purse."

The sound ended after she jabbed him in the thigh, and a tense five minutes passed before any of them were able to release their figurative breaths. A hint of color returned to Tommy's cheeks, overcoming the deathly pallor of a werewolf in his final moments.

"Sorry for causing all this trouble, Riv."

"What? Nah, you didn't cause any trouble. You're actually a better patient than Zac," she teased to lighten the mood. She wiped away old blood, cleansed the wound, and used a few butterfly closures to fasten the skin together. While her hands were steady, she remained relatively unpracticed in administering stitches and hesitated to try. She'd have to convince him to let her call his wife.

"Doesn't take much to make a better patient than Zac," he mumbled. "Still, I owe you for saving my life. Pretty sure that's what you just did."

"You know, with your wife being a veterinarian, she'd probably have done a better job than me."

Tommy shook his head. "You did just fine, Riv. Besides, I don't wanna worry her. She's got enough on her mind."

"Trust me, she'll be more upset she wasn't told."

He gave a weak chuckle then groaned.

"I'm going to call Ceres and Emma, okay, hon?"

"Okay."

River stroked his brow then plucked the cordless from the cradle. A drowsy voice greeted her after five rings. "Hello?"

"Ceres?"

"Yeah? Who's asking?" A bed creaked and a softer voice in the background asked who was on the phone. The girls must have been asleep.

"It's River Jackson. Tommy is here at my place."

Ceres sighed. "Did he drink too much to drive home? I'll come get h—"

"No, no. That's not necessary. I'm not kicking him out…" River hesitated. "There was an attack at the Sin Den tonight and Tommy was injured. By a silver blade."

"What?" Ceres asked in a sharp, alert tone.

"I gave him an antidote for it, and he's resting in our spare bedroom."

"We'll be right there." The line disconnected before River could respond.

When the ladies arrived twenty minutes later in their husband's truck, the guys had already taken off on foot to retrieve Bobby's ratty old van from Tommy's driveway. The two women were as different as night and day. Ceres was tall, lean, and golden blonde. At six months of pregnancy, the baby bump stretching her yoga pants and camisole had become the most prominent curve on her. By comparison, Emma was short and full figured, a Native American woman with dark eyes and glossy, straight black hair.

"How is he?" Emma beat Ceres to the question.

"He's fine now, he's fine. I swear. We caught it in time, so I gave him a sleep-aid for the pain." Once River described the rest of the on-the-fly treatment, Emma nodded in appreciation and Ceres hugged her in a bone-crushing embrace.

"Thank you. Thank you for saving our Tommy. Thank you."

"No need to thank me," River squeaked. "Except for letting me breathe a little maybe."

Ceres released her at once and choked back a sob. "Sorry. I just... All these hormones get me so emotional now. I could just... could just *skin him* for trying to hide it from us."

No skinning was done, but the two women did tearfully hug and kiss their werewolf husband. They stroked his dark hair, caressed his pale cheeks, and made him promise to never keep an illness secret from them again. Drowsily, Tommy agreed to everything they asked before River and Zac slipped from the room and shut the door behind them.

"That was close. Even if you had taken him to the hospital, I don't think they would have known what to do," River whispered once they were upstairs in their own bedroom.

Zac slid into place behind her and wrapped his arms around her waist. "Maybe those people in California have the right idea about bringing all of us out into the open. Would be nice if werewolves could drop by the hospital ER like any other person." Last they'd heard, there were rumors about a dragon in California wanting to run for governor, and if that happened, how long would it be until he also suggested bringing their world out into the open?

"Maybe. But then us witches will be harassed to death once people realize mystics and fortune tellers are real. 'Tell me my fortune', 'who was I in my past life?', 'does so and so like me?', and anything else they can think of asking."

"Fuck that," Zac said. "I don't want to know my secret crush; I want you to tell me tomorrow's winning lotto numbers."

She mock-scowled at him, but he'd made her laugh, which she imagined was the goal.

CHAPTER 4

A t least twice a month, River and Pythia met for brunch in the older woman's backyard. They'd adjusted the time of their meetings during the sweltering months of summer, beginning tea time at 9:00 a.m. before the sun's full intensity was upon them.

Some of the most beautiful gardens in the world flourished in the backyards of witches. River had a green thumb, but even she envied the masterpiece spanning acres across her best friend's property. Flowers and herbs of every variety grew in abundance, with narrow trails woven between them for visiting witches to safely travel without trampling the fragrant growth.

Nearer to the home, flowers and herbs spilled from colorful pots, filled carefully plotted beds, and twined up wooden arches. A fat bumblebee buzzed from plant to plant while hummingbirds darted around a cluster of columbine. Every basic item a proper alchemist needed could be found in Pythia's sanctuary.

And not a single mosquito. That alone made River envious.

Morning glories and sweet tea roses covered the gazebo where they drank tea. River loved the cozy shelter

Pythia's human father had constructed for her, and Zacarias had promised to build one for her over the summer.

After tiptoeing around the news of recent developments in the coven and her enjoyment of her productive new title, River blurted out the real question on her mind. "Have you ever had to deal with vampires?"

Pythia snapped her attention from the centerpiece. "Vampires?"

"The guys had an encounter with them last night. One of Zac's shifter friends almost died."

She decided not to mention her strange brewing epiphany, afraid of how Pythia would take it. Afraid it meant something more than being a brilliant prodigy when it came to the cauldron. As far as they both knew, River's current life was her first lifetime as a witch and she wasn't a reincarnated sorceress like her mentor. Yet.

"How many vampires?" Pythia fixed her with a decidedly curious look.

"Four. One big guy and three females, I think he said. Plus their thralls."

"And where did the boys run afoul of these vampires?"

River sighed. "The strip club. They all visit the strip club once a month for kicks and to hang out. Do guy stuff. So they were throwing their money away when Zac and Tommy noticed their stripper was a vampire. Then they realized they were all alone. It was like…"

"A setup?" Pythia asked.

River nodded. "His wife drove him home this morning once his supernatural healing kicked in, but he still looked awful."

"What I'm about to tell you has to stay just between us, all right? You cannot share this with Zacarias yet, or his friends, especially Tommy, until we have the rest of the details. We don't want the shifter community on our backs."

River leaned forward, growing increasingly intrigued as Pythia stirred a sense of mystery around the subject. There had always been secrets among the witches, but rarely was it ever spelled out so plainly. "You have my word I won't mention it to anyone."

"Someone performed a Blood Sacrament last night at the Atropos Recreation Center."

River gasped, the news as shocking as diving naked into a frigid lake. "No…" She pressed her knuckles against her lips and stared. "With what? Not a…"

"A child," Pythia confirmed. "And his mother."

Nausea welled within her and threatened to upheave the fine brunch she'd enjoyed. "No," she whispered through tears. "That's horrible."

A Blood Sacrament wasn't only a murder; it was a violation of the soul. Dark witches resorted to them on occasion for the surge of raw, unfiltered power that came from a soul as fresh as a child's.

After a sorrowful shake of her head, Pythia refilled their mugs and pushed one toward her. If the older witch's famous lemon and ginger tea wouldn't settle River's turbulent stomach, nothing would.

River managed a few sips before she was able to voice a question. "Was it a kid from Atropos?"

Pythia nodded. The tight grip on the handle of her tea mug betrayed her calm exterior. "It was Jack Wiggins."

River's mug slipped free and clattered to the wooden gazebo floor. If any pair could be a set of best friends to the community, it was Jack and his mother, Pam. The sweetest woman she'd ever met and a child she'd once babysat were gone forever. She couldn't move, numbed to the core, her flesh chilled with goose bumps as her mind crawled over the steps of the horrific act.

"Now you understand why I invited you to brunch. I wanted to tell you before you could learn about the incident in some other way," Pythia murmured. "It grieves me to share the news, River."

Mute at first, she nodded and wiped at her cheeks with her hands. It took time to find her voice. "Murder in Atropos is a big damned deal, Pythia. What are the police going to—"

"The police arrested Pam's ex-husband."

"Joe? But… No, I can't believe it. Are the police sure it was him?"

"They didn't have any choice in the matter because the circumstantial evidence points to him. We know better, and the chief knows better, but there's nothing we can do about it right now."

"Joe is harmless. He was kind of a layabout when they were married, but he wouldn't have hurt Pam or Jack. He *loved* his son. I drove past them fishing at the creek a week ago."

Pythia raised one shoulder in a meek shrug. "And now he's behind bars for atrocities we both know he wouldn't commit against his ex-wife and son. I doubt the DNA evidence recovered from Pam will point at him, but their rocky relationship and all of the public arguments are stacked against him."

Fresh tears welled over River's lashes. "Then there's a male warlock around," she said.

Pythia nodded. "Or a woman like Lucia with an immoral piece of shit for a boyfriend."

"Possibly the very same warlock Lucia worked alongside in October." River rubbed her arms. "She cried out for someone in the shadows to help her, but they abandoned her like they didn't care."

"Warlocks rarely care for the well-being of their failed disciples. There's a chance it could be the same one. The things I would do to him if I could only track him down with a little magic. Unfortunately, the ones responsible for it are professionals in that sense and left behind very few clues."

Fresh tears sprang to River's eyes despite her attempts to push the abhorrent images from her mind. "We know what the police did about it, but what are the Texas covens going to do? It's at our back door."

"Sweetheart, it's not at our back door. It's in our home," Pythia said in a quiet voice. "We don't have any choice but to find the ones responsible for it and bind them. There's nothing else that we can do in this situation."

River nodded, but her heart remained with Pam and Jack. By focusing on her final memories of them, she tried to immortalize their smiling faces instead of the grisly images her imagination conjured.

"Aside from gently breaking the news of their deaths to you, I called you here for another reason. We want you to find out who did this. Someone close to home is practicing the darkest of magics, and it cannot be allowed."

"*Me?*" River struggled with the impossible task placed on her shoulders.

Senior witches usually received the most difficult tasks, so when it came to issues related to misuse of magic and murder, their leaders appointed the jobs to girls who had been around the block three or four lifetimes.

Pythia nodded. "After your encounter with Lucia, both the Circle of Seven *and* the Trinity feel like you're ready for the responsibility. I'll do the investigation if you're not up for it yet, but this is the only way to test you and determine if you're ready to become a true sorceress."

For the Circle of Seven to approve meant that the seven most powerful witches in Texas had given their blessing for her to ascend to the next rank in their hierarchy. Recent heartbreak over the loss of Pam and Jack dampened the feeling of success and stole her joy.

"I don't know what to say," River murmured in a hoarse whisper.

"Say you'll put your best effort forward. These people need to be found and punished before they can kill again."

Maybe she couldn't celebrate the promotion, but she could promise to do her best. After clearing her throat, River asked in a level voice, "Do I really have to keep it from Zac? Lying to him isn't really something I want to do. He'll know something is bothering me."

"If you believe Zac can be trusted, then he's allowed to know more. I imagine it's only a matter of time anyway before one of the shifters sniffs around and discovers it. There's too many wolves in Atropos." Pythia tucked a few wisps of her golden-blonde hair behind her ear, the strands escaping her usual single braid. "They're like dogs gnawing on a bone once they realize they've been kept out of a secret."

Her bad pun brought a weak smile to River's face. "Maybe that's part of the problem. We have all this secret-keeping going down, but what we really need is teamwork."

"Perhaps the responsibility of sharing this news should fall to you then."

"Wait, what?" River's eyes darted to her in a panic as she imagined rounding up the leaders of the shifter groups. "Why me?"

A sly smile raised the corners of Pythia's mouth. "Who better to become acting liaison between our circle and the shifters than you, since you've developed such an interest in their affairs."

Jerk.

"Fine. I'll set up a meeting with them after I've done some preliminary research."

"A wise plan."

"What about Lucia?" River asked. "Have you considered restoring her to a human form and questioning her for info, just in case it *is* the same warlock she helped last year?"

Pythia almost choked on her tea, the sip interrupted by a sharp, bitter laugh. "No, certainly not. I see her in her cage each day and while I'm absolutely certain she's plotting revenge, the Trinity has decreed she will remain bound to her animal form for the complete sentence. Then they will reverse her accidental transformation."

They concluded the usual tea time an hour later, Pythia to report to their superiors and River to visit the scene of the crime. She'd have to call the chief and let him know she planned to swing around for a look at the magical print left behind. Viewing that was the last thing she wanted to do, but Pam and Jack deserved justice.

While idling in Pythia's driveway, she dialed up the station and waited for their sole dispatcher to pick up the call.

"Hello, Atropos Police Department. How may I help you?"

"I'd like to speak to Chief Haverton please."

"Who may I say is calling?"

"River Jackson, and I have some information for him about last night's incident."

"Please hold."

It took less than thirty seconds for the line to be picked up, and the chief's gruff voice rumbled across the line. "Listen, River, I can't give out any—"

"I've been assigned to help, Chief," she cut in. "Consider me your magical liaison for the duration of this investigation."

The line quieted long enough for her to glance at the phone to see if they had been disconnected. "Oh. You're one of them. Well then, in that case, what can I do for you? I've been up all night, and we still don't have many leads."

After she explained her needs, Haverton invited her to join him at the scene in two hours, giving her enough time to swing by the house to gather her tools. She pulled into the drive and parked her homely little four-door sedan beside Zac's Jaguar. The shop must have dropped it off first thing with a new tire.

His voice reached her as she stepped inside. "Hey, I gotta go. She just got home, man. Talk to you later."

One look at his dark and brooding eyes was enough to know he'd caught wind of the news around town, probably from Harrison. Gossip was what ravens did best. "Hey... I've been trying to call you for a few."

"I must have hit a bad zone, because my phone never rang." Residents of Atropos were lucky to even have reception in the middle of nowhere.

"Would you like to come in and sit with me for a moment, baby? I have... some bad news I need to share with you."

"I already know." Her soft voice made him stop and blink. "Pythia told me what happened."

"Then is it true that there's magic involved? Harrison is spreading the word."

"It is, but I can't say much more than that. Not right now, at least. I promise to explain more when I get back."

His brows shot up. "Back from where?"

"I'm going out to the recreation center to meet Chief Haverton."

"Then I'm coming with you."

"You don't have to do that."

Zac crossed over and cupped her cheeks between his warm palms, his touch the very thing she needed. Her eyes burned with unshed tears stinging beneath her lids. "I'm not going to let you face that alone. I'll stay out of your way for whatever you need to do, but I'm going to be right there at your side in case you need me."

The floodgates opened as memories of Pam and Jack resurfaced in her thoughts. The occasional glass of wine with Pam. The little boy who came to her door during the summers while his mother taught summer school. He'd grown into a handsome young man. Fifteen was too young to die

Zac kissed her brow. "I love you too much to allow you to face everything alone, River. You remember that. No matter what these witches throw at you, I'll always be here."

With each tear he wiped away, she became more certain that sharing the news with Zacarias was the right thing to do.

She couldn't do anything but nod at first, the tension in her throat too tight for forming words.

Zac didn't rush her. He held her instead and circled his palm up and down her back until the last shudders were over and she whispered a pitiful, "Thanks."

"*De nada.* Besides, maybe you could use my nose. Or Tommy—"

"I may need Tommy, but not yet. Actually, can you call him and Harrison, as well as any other shifter leaders while I'm inside performing my reading?"

"Yeah. Sure thing. What do you want me to tell them?"

"For now, tell them we need to talk as a group. I don't want any specifics mentioned until I actually have, well, specifics. So maybe see if they can all agree to a meetup this week, as soon as tomorrow if they can."

"I can do that."

***

Waiting around outside while his girlfriend faced horror inside the recreation center left Zac feeling helpless, but there was little he could do. River needed an empty space to do the reading without additional auras ruining her magical observation.

Still, he didn't like it. The sharp metallic scent of blood lingered in the area, strongest whenever the front door swung open and shut again. The chief of police stepped outside and mopped his brow with a handkerchief from his pocket before sliding his wraparound shades on again.

"Hell of a mess, all this. I, uh, hate to ask you, Zac, but do you think you could, uh, sniff around out here any? We've combed through the grass, and I don't suspect there's much else here human eyes can find. Whoever did it was like a ghost. The only physical evidence left behind belonged to the victims."

Damn.

Occasionally, Zac wished he had an animal form common to the area, something less exotic than the black jaguar shape he'd inherited from his Brazilian parents.

If he prowled around the building perimeter the way he wanted to, some country local would probably notice from his pickup truck and get trigger happy.

He had to rely on his human nose instead, senses heightened but imperfect.

"I'll do what I can. It's okay for me to walk around?"

Haverton swept his wrist across his perspiring brow. The sun had come out in full force and raised the temperature to the mid-nineties. "Yeah, sure. If you find something, just don't touch it, and give me a holler."

"Of course, sir."

Lingering scents marked the area, everything from humans to the raccoons who ransacked the trash cans after dark. At first, he thought it would be impossible to single out the perpetrator, because too many familiar smells assaulted him at once, the sheer combination of people entering and exiting the area on a typical weekend creating an amalgam of Atropos's residents.

As Zac crossed beside a window, the cloying, honeysuckle odor of vampire wafted past him on a breeze. Each shifter perceived their particular "aroma" differently.

Tommy thought vampires smelled like puke. Harrison claimed the smell reminded him of birthday cake, and then later regretted mentioning it since the gang spent the rest of the night making jokes about his appetite, corvid diets, and road kill, even though real vampires weren't actually dead.

Dead vamps all had the same stench though; they reeked of sour bile and wood ashes.

Tracking the vampire's path across the adjacent playground led to the road where the scent vanished, and he encountered the black streaks of tire marks stretched across the ground.

While Zacarias debated whether or not it was a coincidence, Chief Haverton strolled up behind him.

"You find somethin', son?"

"Maybe," Zac said. "Could be nothing. Could be the getaway car's tracks. You gotta figure someone was waiting on standby to get the killer away after they were done."

"I'll call in some help from the county on this then. The marks are fresh." Haverton pulled a digital camera from his pocket and snapped a few photographs before he stepped away to make a call on his phone.

Zac left the chief with the evidence and circled back around to the recreation center's front entrance doors. Tinted glass and a dark atmosphere within concealed River's activities.

Another half hour ticked by before the door opened and River emerged. One look at her pale face and trembling hands summoned every protective instinct Zac possessed. Reaching her in a few quick steps, he took her in his arms and held her against his chest.

"I'm okay," she lied in a whispered breath. "I need to talk to the chief."

"Shh. You can tell him whatever you saw tomorrow. Right now, I'm taking you home and running you a bath."

"No. No, I need to do this now. Okay?" Contrary to her brave words, River's fingers curled into his shoulders for support.

"You sure?"

"Positive. It's what they sent me here to do."

Once he'd held her long enough for the shudders to subside, he caught her up on the discovery made while she performed magic inside. Her chin raised and her honey-colored eyes widened.

"That makes sense, because I found traces of blood magic inside. Not the ordinary kind. Literally performed on their blood as it was drained from them."

"What would make a warlock team up with vampires though?"

"That's what Pythia wants me to find out." She shivered again, but waved him off when he tried to draw her away to the car. "I have to do this. You can coddle me once we're home. I promise."

Respecting her wishes, he followed her across the park ground to the chief. Dusty had settled at a picnic table to await the news. He took it better than expected.

"You need to be careful on this one, Dusty," River said in a low voice, using the chief's first name. "We're dealing with some really black magic here. And..."

"And what?"

"Vampires. Right now, until we can figure out why there are vampires involved, the best and safest place for Joe is in the lockup where you have him."

"You think he might be targeted?"

"Magic as foul as this tends to be more potent when a whole bloodline is used. You're taking something beautiful, the ties of family, and corrupting it. If they want more power, they'll go for him next."

The grim-faced chief ran his fingers through his thinning gray hair. He wasn't yet fifty, but Zac imagined years of dealing with shifter mayhem had taken its toll on him. According to Harrison and Tommy, the chief had been in the know for a long while.

"All right. I swear, it's something new with you folk every time I turn around. What do I need to know about vampires? What's fact and what's fiction? Do I need to get folks off the street and encourage Mayor Johnson to set some kind of curfew in place?"

"They can't walk in the sun," River said. "That's one of the legends with some truth to it."

"They don't turn into wolves and bats," Zac offered. "But the elders can become fog and mist."

Haverton pulled a crucifix from inside his uniform shirt. "What about this?"

"They're not undead, and they're not actual demons," River explained. "At least, we haven't proven that they are yet. I've heard of religious icons causing discomfort before, but it really varies from vampire to vampire. I think it's the faith and the belief in it working, not, you know… an actual force from any deity."

Zac nodded in agreement. "The ones born into it are even tougher though, from what I've heard. Home in Brazil, they're far worse than anything I've heard about in America. Easier for them to terrorize villages away from the city."

"Fuck. Those things can breed?"

"Rarely. They seem to prefer turning adults." River's eyes darted toward the arrival of more law enforcement vehicles. Atropos wasn't equipped to handle big-time forensics like this. "The jail and your dominion over it is the most powerful weapon you have right now to keep Joe safe. They can't enter where they're not permitted, and since the cells are off limits, that means no one can get to Joe."

"All right. Garlic?"

"Only good for flavoring dishes," Zac replied sadly. "So don't count on it helping you."

"Probably for the best. The place stinks enough." The chief sighed. "All right, you two head on home now. I'll finish up here and make sure we're cleared out before dark. If you discover anything else about this, holler at me."

"Of course," River said with a forced smile on her face. "About the curfew you mentioned—it's a good idea. Kids are never on the menu in a typical coven, but if these are rogues, they're not guaranteed to follow the rules."

"Gotcha. I'll have a word with the mayor and convince him we need to enact a 9:00 p.m. curfew until further notice."

On the outside, River appeared reserved and calm, but Zacarias had a year of experience to learn the subtleties of her moods. Her tense shoulders and the squint to her eyes alluded to one of her tension headaches. She was barely holding it together, and once they crossed the stretch of green grass to return to his Jag, she sagged against the seat.

"Home?" he asked, giving her the benefit of the doubt.

"No, not home. We need to head toward Bandera on the other side of San Antonio. I'll give you directions along the way."

He sighed. "What's the plan?"

"To see the vampire leaders and report a crime, because the longer we wait to see them, the more time the bad ones will have to get their story together."

CHAPTER 5

Most witches knew where to find the rest of the big supernatural players in their region. As collectors of knowledge and secrets, they made it their business to know how to locate the shifter leaders, vampires, and all the other paranormal creatures.

The vampires lived on the northwestern outskirts of San Antonio on a centuries-old plantation, accessible only by a narrow farm road bordered by mountains carpeted by trees. The setting sun shone fiery red just above the forest, a reminder of the inconvenient time of the day for visiting the bloodsuckers.

And because of his distrust for their kind, Zac refused to let her go alone.

"Who are we chatting with again? Dracula?"

She sighed. "No. We're meeting with Rosenhaven's master of liaisons, Felicity. She's like a vampire diplomat."

According to what River learned as a child from her sorceress mother, Felicity instructed the vampire neophytes in the rules and represented their coven during meetings.

River had only met the liaison once, back when her powers first emerged at puberty and she received her first spellbook. Because the council held coming-out parties for young witches—debutante balls without the dancing—it wasn't uncommon to receive gifts from the other supernaturals.

Argus Prescott, Tommy's father-in-law and the original alpha over the local San Antonio werewolf pack, had gifted her a planter of wolfbane. The vamps, not to be outdone, had given the young witch her first silver knife, which she still used while chopping ingredients for the cauldron.

While Argus hadn't recognized her as an adult when she moved back into town, she'd never forgotten the kindness he'd shown her as a shy teenage witch. Likewise, it startled her that the vampires who were once so charming and gracious, had become boorish recluses who no longer honored the old ways.

Her mother said she could always trust Felicity to do the right thing. While she wasn't a dark witch, Cynthia Jackson was more gray or neutral, and she'd introduced her daughter to some interesting people while River was growing up. Felicity wasn't Cynthia's strangest friend, and she still kept unusual company.

Because Felicity hadn't accepted any recent calls from Cynthia, River had been forced to make the visit in person. If her mother hadn't already been on her way to enjoy a Norwegian cruise with her current boyfriend, she'd have accompanied her.

She'd practically had to beg her mom not to cancel her plans and turn around from the airport.

Zac glanced over out of the corner of his eye as they cruised toward the vampire coven's plantation. "Are you sure you want to do this? Why don't we just Skype with them instead and save ourselves having to smell the rot on them?"

"Tell me how you really feel about vampires. They're not even dead," she groaned.

"I'm just sayin'. I mean, it's still daylight. Kind of. They'd probably appreciate getting some more sleep…"

"Better to face this now," she said. "Besides, they wouldn't dare hurt me. Felicity may be ignoring our calls, but she *is* a family friend. Plus, I'm the official ambassador from our circle, and everyone knows I'm here. If I don't check in after this, every witch and sorcerer from here to Houston will come down on their complex. Pythia said they'd even pay Saul Drakenstone's price and get the dragons involved, and no one wants that."

Zac shuddered. "I like to consider myself a brave man, but meeting them is terrifying. Absolutely pants-wetting terrifying."

"I've never met a dragon, and to be honest with you, I'm fine keeping it that way."

"But you're okay with meeting vampires. At least dragons don't eat people anymore."

"They can't help what they need to survive. *Some* of them are good people."

An immense white house arose from the top of a green hill in the distance, lit by the fading orange glow of the descending sun. Zac slowed to a stop before the wrought iron gate and lowered his window to buzz in.

"State your business," a bored voice asked through the intercom.

River leaned across the center console. "I'm here to speak with Felicity. The Daughters of the Moon should have called ahead and made the arrangements."

The intercom went silent and the gates swung open, allowing them onto the property. They swung shut behind them with unspoken finality, and she wondered if Zac's car could burst through them, or if a Jag could even outrun a vamp at all.

Negative on both counts probably.

The road continued for another half mile before curving around a tall stone fountain sending up streams of water in graceful arcs. Once Zac parked at the edge closest to the mansion, they left the vehicle and traveled a stepping-stone path across an immense green lawn.

"Last chance to turn back," she whispered to him, wondering if the vamps could see their approaching mortal guests. Glancing up, she noticed a tinted glass dome positioned on the porch's overhang. They were on candid vamp-cam.

"Not sending you in alone."

River knocked on the door. It gave on the second thump of her knuckles, creaking as it swung inward to reveal a dimmed foyer lit more by lights than the sun. Vamps constructed their homes with special, sun-shielded glass to protect them from its rays during daylight.

"Yeah, cause that's not creepy at all," he muttered under his breath.

"Let's take comfort in knowing we aren't in a horror movie."

"You sure about that?"

Having Zac alongside her changed everything, and although she had faith in her safety regardless of whether or not he was present, she still appreciated the support—that he'd overcome his own natural fear of bloodsuckers to escort her through the snake pit.

Zac's fingers remained on her arm, his touch persistent even as they moved through the vacant foyer. Once the door shut, an audible click echoed through the room as the locks snapped into place behind them. Zac's eyes narrowed.

It's a precaution, she told herself, trying to convince her brain it was all a matter of not accidentally allowing the daylight in.

Except it was past sundown.

They stood alone in a sprawling foyer filled with art and old marble busts. A magnificent chandelier dangled from the ceiling, glittering with a few dozen crystals and radiant bulbs. The golden hardwood oak beneath their feet stretched across the space to a split staircase. There were doors to the left and right, but no people to greet them.

"Having doubts about the horror movie thing," Zac whispered in her ear. He didn't release her, his skepticism growing by the second and filtering through their link.

"Welcome to our home," a jubilant voice cried from above.

River glanced up to the second-floor railing to see a woman smiling down at them.

Like most supernatural creatures, vampires resembled models posing for fashion shoots in Paris, or actors on the silver screen. The woman who came to receive them was no different, dressed like she'd stepped off a runway. Taupe silk hugged her slim waist and cascaded down to her feet. A long slit in the flowing skirt revealed a slender leg up to her thigh. Her dark hair framed her face in enviable, sleek waves.

When the vampiress glided down the stairs as if she were more wraith than woman, Zac squeezed River's arm tighter, bruising her.

"Welcome to Rosenhaven," she reaffirmed once she stood before them. "I am Lady Margot Calloway."

With a phony smile plastered on her face, River inclined her head in a polite nod. "Thank you. I'm River Jackson, and I've come on behalf of the Daughters of the Moon. I expected Felicity to greet me."

"Felicity is no longer with us."

"No longer with you?"

Margot sighed. "Afraid not, dearest. Now who is this exemplary specimen of a man? A gift for us? My word, the witches haven't honored the old traditions in so long I had wondered if they had forgotten them altogether."

Zac tensed and a low growl rumbled in his chest. Margot only smiled.

"Ah, your bodyguard. Pity, he would make a nice pet. I have a fondness for cats."

In the name of diplomacy, River ignored the slight against her boyfriend, although she made a mental note to make it up to him later. She cleared her throat instead and raised her chin to meet Margot's hungry gaze head on. "When you say Felicity is no longer with you, do you mean…?"

"She died, sweet. Terrible tragedy. A great loss to our coven," she drawled, her voice reminiscent of a southern belle from an old civil war film.

Her words splashed ice water on River's courage. She faltered and blinked. "Dead? But... *How?*"

"An awful mishap with the shutters of the aviary. It was one of her favorite places to visit, you see, though we had yet to replace the glass..." She gave them a small, tight smile, revealing too much fang. "Perhaps you would prefer to speak with our new master of liaisons?"

"Or I can talk with you."

Margot laughed, the sound light and musical. "Oh no, honey, that isn't how it works."

"There are strong allegations against your coven, Madame Calloway—"

"Then I am certain you and Tremaine can work them out. I will send him down."

Margot brushed River off and swept away into the next room. The door clicked shut behind her with a resounding echo.

Zac opened his mouth, but River touched one finger to her lips and whispered a gentle, "Shh." Her gaze darted to the pair of cameras angled toward them from the ceiling.

They waited instead, on pins and needles. The sensation of being under surveillance never faded no matter how much she tried to avoid looking at the cameras.

"Greetings," a man's voice called from their right.

They swung around to face the source of the mysterious voice. Apparently even Zac, with his superior sense of smell and hearing, hadn't noticed the vampire's arrival. When he jerked around, he also stumbled back a step while shoving River behind him. Vampires moved like ghosts. Scary, blood-drinking ghosts.

"Apologies," the vampire said. He stood a couple inches shorter than Zacarias, his head shaven bald and facial hair groomed into a tidy goatee around a full, seductive mouth. He would have been the kind of man to suit her tastes if she didn't have her panther, and if he weren't a bloodthirsty supernatural creature. "I am Tremaine Montgomery, master of liaisons in this house."

"River Jackson," she replied, still shaking. "And my boyfriend, Zacarias Silva."

"River Jackson... Jackson. Quite a familiar name. In fact, your face—"

"My dad is Ronny 'Earthquake' Jackson," she replied in a dull tone, accustomed to occasionally meeting her father's old fans.

The vampire grinned, showing all his perfectly aligned white teeth. They gleamed beneath eyes the color of fine cognac. "Ah yes, of course. The years have been kind since you were a little girl visiting your father at the stadium. What a pleasure to meet you now as an adult, Miss Jackson. Please join me in the dining room. I hope you don't mind that I've arranged for refreshments."

He gestured to the door behind him then led the way through rooms of increasing beauty and elegance, the old charm of the forgotten southern era restored by touches of modern convenience.

The formal room had a regal feel about it. A crystal chandelier hung from the center of the ceiling over a long, polished oak table. River's attention drifted to a stylish antique cabinet on the back wall holding a gorgeous display of bone china. She coveted it immediately, much like the rest of the house she'd seen so far.

Once everyone took their seats, Tremaine poured coffee. Lacking shame, Zac raised River's cup and sniffed its contents before letting her have a sip.

If Tremaine noticed, he didn't let it show. He smiled instead. "Now, what may I do for you, friends?"

"First, allow me to offer my sympathies regarding Felicity's death. My mother introduced me to her once. From what I remember of her and the things Mom has said, Felicity was a good woman."

"Thank you. I hope, in time, I will be able to forge an equally stable relationship with your council as she did. So please, tell me, what brings you to Rosenhaven?"

"There have been two attacks in the past week involving vampires."

"We had nothing to do with those."

Her brows rose. "I haven't even said when or where."

Tremaine's fangs shone against his dark skin when he smiled. He'd probably had a complexion like rich milk chocolate during his human life, but a subtle unearthly sheen had robbed him of the warmth. "Our coven has no association with *any* attacks, Miss Jackson."

"Someone was certainly responsible. Zacarias witnessed an attack at the Sin Den." She paused, giving it enough time to sink in before adding, "And helped stop it."

"I killed many vampires," Zac said, hitting the point home. "*Many.*"

"As I was told by Argus Prescott when he phoned to make his complaints. I'm afraid there's nothing we can do, however, as that incident was beyond our jurisdiction." Tremaine's amber eyes glinted. "I considered the matter to be closed since justice had been dealt."

"Isn't it your job to oversee the vampires in the area?" Zac asked.

"We cannot account for every rogue vampire that migrates through Texas. As I'm sure you shifters and witches often have your own vagabonds to deal with," he said in a smooth jazz baritone.

"We certainly do. I have reason to believe a warlock and several vampires are responsible for a Blood Sacrament in Atropos, Texas. Which means this coven is obligated to lend their aid in the search for the perpetrators. By the will of the Daughters of the Moon, I am hereby informing you of this coven's responsibility. The Circle of Seven finds Rosenhaven accountable."

The smile faded from Tremaine's face at last, replaced by a stoic mask. "That is a serious accusation."

"A true one. At least two vampires were present when a young boy and his mother were murdered last night. This points to a potentially lasting problem in the area."

By using the power of the council and invoking the covenant between the two supernatural groups, Tremaine didn't have a chance of bowing out. Keeping the satisfaction off her face, River matched his expression with an indifferent mask of her own.

Zac didn't even try. He grinned from ear to ear.

"Very well. I must consult with the other masters. Your council will be notified once we have assigned a squad of our finest vampire knights to assist with your investigation."

"Appreciated," she replied.

Tremaine rose from the seat. "If you'll excuse me, there are important matters requiring my attention."

The vampire liaison escorted them back to the front door. The coven had come alive during the course of the meeting, and immortal beauties glided by while shooting inquisitive, even ravenous, glances.

River fixed a brunette with a hard stare for watching Zac too closely in the corridor. She sniffed and carried on her way.

"When may I expect your response?" she asked the master. They stood before the cream-colored double entrance doors, both open to reveal night had fallen completely.

"By dawn," Tremaine said.

Before she could thank him for his time, he was gone.

CHAPTER 6

The shifters needed time to assemble. Tremaine's excuses, or rather his failure to voluntarily offer aid after the attack, had pissed Argus off enough to call in big friends from East Texas.

Zacarias didn't envy River's position either. The shifter clans wanted answers, and she hadn't satisfied their demands to know more, so he acted as a go-between to soothe Argus and his friends when they initiated a three-way call at the crack of dawn.

River had only fallen asleep thirty minutes earlier after ending a phone call with Tremaine. She'd spent the entire night reading, researching, and tapping witch contacts for information about blood rituals. By the time Zac ushered her to bed, she had looked like a zombie.

"I promise, she's going to tell you everything. She's tired though, and I'm not going to drag her out of bed. Sorry, Ian."

The eagle shifter on the other end chuckled. "That's no problem. Either way, I'm bringing a friend along with me from Quickdraw. Should only be a couple hours before we arrive. We're already on the road."

"I'll be sure to have the coffee going," Argus said. "Please join us as early as possible, Zac."

He spent a moment longer on the line with the two gentlemen, promised he and River would be there by lunchtime at the latest, then hung up and tossed the phone aside.

With a few hours' leeway, he set the alarm on his phone and crashed on the couch. The four hours helped. Not much, but they helped.

To rouse River from bed, he brewed a pot of extra strong coffee in her favorite flavor. The Kahlua and caramel aroma lured her down the stairs.

"Well look at that. Looks like I don't need magic spells to summon you," Zac called.

"Uggggh, I feel and look like shit," she complained. She leaned closer to a mirror in the hall outside of the kitchen, checking out the circles beneath her eyes. "Why do you look so good when you didn't go to bed until I did?"

"I napped on and off, remember? It's what we cats do. Anyway, I scored you a meeting with the bigwig shifters, so you have thirty to shower and be ready to roll to Prescott Manor."

"Ugh. Fine. Can you pour my coffee in a travel mug?"

"Already done."

Forty-five minutes later, they were on the road. River chugged her coffee and stared out the window without her usual chatter. Zac glanced over twice to see if she'd fallen back asleep, but each time, she only stared mournfully out the window.

He wanted to be angry at the council of witches for pinning her with an impossible task, but he couldn't resent them for long. River was right; every paranormal being had some degree of responsibility for dealing with the troubles in their world.

"Ready for this?"

"Shifters are preferable to vamps," she replied. "At least most of you guys won't eat me."

Prescott Manor sat in the middle of a hundred acres of private land, perfect for a pack of wolves to roam and hunt. There wasn't much to see but trees on either side of the long drive and Tommy's truck parked beside an unfamiliar black SUV with an enormous, glossy grille guard and a protected bumper to match. Clothed in cargo shorts and a T-shirt stretched taut over his enormous muscles, Tommy waved from his seat on the porch swing. He rose when they parked.

"You look way better, man," Zac said as he climbed out.

"Yeah, well, that's what happens when you have two women threatening to fillet you if you get outta bed." Tommy laughed and ran a hand through his hair. "Harrison's not far behind you. He went to pick up the bear representative."

"Should we head inside then?" River turned her tired gaze toward the front door.

Tommy shook his head. "Do you really wanna get pounced before he gets here? I get that it takes time for y'all to come up with information, but Argus is in there chomping at the bit to have answers."

"No, not really."

They opted to take Tommy's advice and linger on the porch instead, hanging with him until Harrison arrived in his Chevy. A Native American woman stepped down from the passenger side of the massive pickup, dark hair drawn into two plaits and decorated with brown and white owl feathers.

"This is Maiara," Harrison introduced. "Maiara, meet Tommy, Zac, and River. Tommy runs the second wolf pack around here and Zac is sort of a free agent. River is our local witch."

Tommy offered his hand. "Thank you for coming. I know the bears don't really organize the way we wolves do, so I appreciate you taking the time to join us."

"We wish for answers the same as you," she replied. "Attacks like this threaten all of us."

Of the three men awaiting them in the office, Zac only knew Argus personally. The other man, a middle-aged gentleman with feathery white hair, had been in the newspaper as a celebrated Air Force colonel. Ian MacArthur was a legend among the local shifters, the honorary commander who took the lead whenever there was trouble in the paranormal community.

"Good. Everyone is here," Argus said. "Now we can get down to business."

"Or maybe we could all introduce ourselves and know who we're dealing with," Ian suggested. He clapped his hand on the muscled shoulder of a ginger-haired man in oil-stained jeans. "For those of you who don't recognize me, I'm Ian MacArthur. This fellow beside me is Lyle. He's got the best nose in all of Texas, so I asked him to come along and help us hunt down some vampires."

Zac dropped his eyes to Lyle's prosthetic left arm. It gleamed black from elbow to fingertips and made a gentle, mechanical whirring noise each time it shifted, like something out of a science fiction movie.

Everyone went around and introduced themselves before taking seats, starting with Harrison and ending with River. From there, River continued with the accounting of what had happened at the rec center then at Rosenhaven.

"Felicity died," she said bluntly. "And no one seemed to give a damn that she was dead. I don't want to point fingers, but I think something is up at the coven and we need to get to the heart of it."

"The new guy is a smarmy asshole," Zac muttered.

"I spoke with him over the telephone. This Tremaine is old blood from New Orleans." Argus frowned, lips drawing in a taut, straight line. "And an asshole, as Zac said."

River nodded. "An asshole sending two vampires to help us get to the bottom of the attacks in this area. They claim no one from their coven was involved in the situation at the Sin Den or the murder in Atropos."

Maiara pressed her lips in a thin line. "He is sending two vampires to keep an eye on us and to report back to the coven."

"She's right," Harrison agreed. "If it were me, that's what I'd do. I'd want eyes and ears in the area to watch your progress. Is it too late to decline the help?"

"They'll be here at dusk, so yeah."

"Then we'll use it to our advantage," Ian said. "We keep an eye on the pair once they get here and monitor their movements at night. We need raven surveillance in the trees. They'll notice wolves a mile away, so keep your people away from them, Argus."

"And since they can't watch us during the day either," Lyle said, "we got an advantage over 'em there. I'm pretty fast on even a cold trail, so when you want me to get this shit done, just point me to where I gotta start."

"Work your way from the Wiggins residence to the recreation center," Ian said. "We'll meet you there in a few."

Tommy glanced down at his watch. "I'll give him a ride. Pam was regular as clockwork, so I know all the places she and Jack probably went that day. Give you a call if he finds anything."

"What happens after that?" River asked. "I mean, do you go around town sniffing everyone?"

"If that's what it takes. Vamps keep ghouls to do their daytime dirty work, so I'll let Ian put a leash and a service halter on me and we'll get to work." Lyle grinned, then he and Tommy stepped out of the room.

CHAPTER 7

After an exhausting afternoon with the shifters, River and Zac returned home. She had wanted to accompany Tommy, Ian, and Lyle into town, but they convinced her they would be less conspicuous alone. With no other immediate plans, she settled on the couch with a glass of wine and watched Zac putter around the kitchen.

She loved living with a man able to cook a meal from scratch.

With the gentle notes of a classical station playing from the nearby laptop, she sprawled across the couch and shut her eyes. The savory and spicy aroma of chili powder, cilantro, and spiced beef roused her from a catnap about a half hour later. While balancing two plates on his hands, Zac approached with a dish of what smelled like tacos and looked like pasta. And probably tasted like heaven.

River wrapped some around her fork and pushed it into her mouth, letting flavors explode against her tongue in a sublime symphony of Tex-Mex seasoning. Yup. Heaven.

They sat side by side and stuffed their faces without needing to fill the silence with chatter. Afterward, she crawled into his lap and set her cheek against his shoulder.

Her father wanted to know when they were going to get engaged and have a wedding. He didn't care for them living together in the same house, but since he didn't pay the bills, River blew off her daddy's concerns.

Besides, technically the home belonged to River and Zac both. He owned his half of the duplex and she owned hers. They'd only knocked out a few walls and joined them together into one deluxe abode after selling her old appliances during a yard sale. They kept his newer dishwasher and stove, moved her fridge to the garage, and discovered the joy of cooking in a single immense kitchen with infinite counter space.

She loved her home, but more importantly, she loved her jaguar.

"Feeling any better?" Zac asked.

She shook her head. "I don't know where to begin."

And she also wanted her man to hold her a little longer. Soaking in the warmth from his body, she nuzzled her face against his throat. He wore a cologne she'd made for his birthday, the natural scent of him twined with fragrant herbs and smoky spices. Sighing, she breathed him in and closed her eyes.

There was no comfort more satisfying than Zac's arms. Except for maybe strawberry cheesecake ice cream with molten caramel fudge. Unfortunately, her off-and-on attempts to diet meant there wasn't an ounce in the freezer.

"You know I'll do whatever I can to help you here, Riv. Just tell me whatever you need and I'll do it."

"I know."

Her mind trailed to Joe and Pam. Last she'd heard, they were working on fixing their relationship and overcoming the divorce, possibly him moving into the house again. Now they'd never have their happily ever after.

It made her angry enough to cry in frustration, sobbing hot and angry tears against Zac's shoulder while he rubbed his warm hand in soothing circles up and down her back. That helped. Letting it out provided a moment of sweet catharsis.

"I feel bad for Joe," she whispered.

"So do I," Zac replied. "I think he deserves to know why he's in jail and what happened. I had time to think about it, and I know he's a human, but it isn't right, you know? You can't lock a man up for the murder of his own family to keep him safe, but not let him know what you're protecting him from. He's going through a hell we can't ever comprehend, *querida*."

"Agreed. I guess I better do that now."

Zac startled when she rose from his lap. "Now?"

"Yeah. Before bed, and before it's dark too."

A pensive expression flitted over his features before he hid it under the neutral mask she'd come to associate with him having a gripe he didn't want to voice. Hesitant to leave, she cupped a palm against his cheek. "What's wrong?"

"It's nothing."

"It's something. You know you can't hide anything from me."

Zac chuckled and turned his head to kiss her palm. "Don't worry about it. You go and talk to Joe. He needs you more."

"More implies you need me too. What's wrong?"

His exhausted smile barely crinkled the corners of his eyes. "It's stupid. I was kind of hoping to have some time alone with you."

And the truth came out, twisting a knot into her stomach when she realized the recent streak of occurrences and witchy business had taken their private time down to zilch. Crap. Somehow, she'd have to balance being an investigative super-witch and a girlfriend to a good man.

"Backrubs for you when I come back, and then I want to talk to you about something that's been on my mind too. Okay?"

He raised a dark brow. "Okay. Gonna give me a hint?"

"Nope. You'll find out when I'm home."

Any day now, she thought Zacarias planned to propose, and only because of her recent reading with her favorite deck of Oracle cards. According to the message she'd divined from them, her life was soon to undergo an irreversible, profound change. It had to mean marriage.

But marriage wasn't irreversible. Couples across the world divorced every day.

Still, recent changes in Zacarias's typical behavior led her to believe he was ready to pop the question. He'd acquired a possessive, overprotective overtone, like she was already carrying his child. Prior conversations with him had revealed he wanted a whole brood of kids, while River had been reluctant to reveal that witches rarely, if ever, had even one child.

How did she tell him that? Better yet, why was her heart set against them at all?

The time had come for her to do some long overdue soul-searching instead of wondering why Zacarias hadn't yet asked her to marry him. Maybe he'd been waiting for the perfect romantic moment, and for lack of intimate time together, always missed the opportunity. If the loss of Pam and Jack had taught her anything, it was to make every moment with loved ones count. If he wouldn't be the one to bring it up, maybe the time had come to take matters into her own hands.

Unless his manipulative ex-wife had ruined marriage for him altogether. And if that was the case, that was fine.

It's not like I want kids or anything. But… if Zac asked. If we discussed it together….

River shook it off and placed her focus where it belonged. First, she had to help Joe before she could take charge of her own relationship.

***

After parking in front of the Atropos Police Department, River stepped into a tiny, matchbox-sized lobby with three old chairs, a few dusty, phony houseplants, and a vending machine. Photographs, advertisements for local services, wanted posters, and flyers covered the bulletin board beside a tiny window between her and a single dispatcher-slash-receptionist.

Bonnie worked the afternoon shift through most of the week. She waved from a computer at the far side of the room.

"Hey, girl. Is Dusty in?" River asked.

"Hi, River. Yeah. He just went back a few moments ago. You need him?"

"Yes, please."

Once Bonnie buzzed her to the back, River meandered down a carpeted hallway to Dusty's office. The chief sat behind his desk with his feet kicked up and a phone raised to his ear.

"Tell me about it, Gary. I got shifters crawling all over this town now over this nonsense. Vampires murdering schoolteachers and children. Warlocks. I've never seen anything this bad in Atropos."

Gary. The only Gary that sprang to mind right away was Judge McKinley, a member of the raven shifter community, and he already knew about the attacks thanks to Harrison.

She paused in the doorway of the office then stepped back, but Dusty waved her inside and gestured to the empty chair.

"Yeah. We're going to need you to set bail at an unusually high amount. We can't allow him to leave. What? If we let this man out, he's a goner. The vamps will go after him too."

Tension turned her stomach into a queasy mess.

"I know the law says—" He quieted a moment, cut off on the other end. "There has to be a way to hold him longer… Fine. All right. I'll ring you back later. River Jackson is here, and I don't think it's a social call. It's probably about this mess."

She waited for him to end the call before speaking up. "He isn't going to help us keep Joe behind bars, is he?"

Dusty shook his head and spread both hands in a helpless gesture. "I don't think there's anything we can do to keep him locked up. Joe's alibi is shaky, but there's no physical evidence tying him to the crime scene."

"What about the DNA evidence you guys found on Pam?"

"A few strands of hair on her dress from the neighbor's toddler she'd babysat that evening. No prints, no semen, no skin samples. Perp was like a goddamned ghost. We could try to pin motive on Joe since Carl Knox saw them arguing on the lawn a day earlier about having Jack home on time from visits."

"But arguing doesn't mean he came back and killed them in a sadistic ritual," she finished.

"Right."

Crushing guilt fell over her at the thought of Joe out there alone, undefended and helpless in the event of those monsters returning for his blood. She blinked back the tears stinging the corners of her eyes and sucked in a breath.

"We need to tell him the truth. If there's a big chance of him going free, Joe has to know what really happened to Pam and Jack," she said.

"So you want to tell this man that vampires tortured his loved ones?" Dusty asked incredulously.

"Yes. Besides, most vampires tend to strike the people they know first. They'll build a rapport to gain easy access to their victims. Maybe he can shed some light on this entire situation for us. It could be someone he or Pam knew."

"All right. I'll follow your lead on this one." He tossed River a ring with a dozen keys then slouched back in his chair, looking as defeated as she felt.

Poor Dusty. Poor Joe. Poor everybody involved in this mess she was somehow supposed to fix.

"The copper key is to the holding cells. Turn left at the end of the hall."

As a tiny rural town with less than two thousand people, their population didn't require more than the police department's small staff of six officers. They never saw more than two on duty at a time unless there was a BBQ or a party.

A huge steel door barred the way into the holding area, and she was thankful the area smelled clean when she entered. The setting sun shone through a window, casting light over the polished cement floor. To River's left, a row of bars separated her from three cells.

Joe occupied the farthest cell at the end, alone because arrests in their town only happened during domestic disputes or when rowdy drunks behaved out of hand. He sat on the side of a narrow cot with thin sheets and a wool blanket, staring at the cinderblock walls with a vacant expression on his face.

He resembled a zombie, his unshaven face pale with purple smudges beneath his red-rimmed eyes. An untouched tray of dinner was on the floor by the bed. A damned good dinner too. Someone had gone down to Mabel's Diner and fetched him the chicken-fried steak platter with a heaping side of mashed potatoes and creamy butter.

"Hi, Joe." When he didn't respond, she continued. "Mind if we chat for a few?"

"What's there to talk about?"

"About why you're here in this jail cell."

He jerked his gaze up to her and stared. "About why they're being nice to me despite what they say I done? They say I murdered them, River. Say I k-killed Pam. They know I couldn't have ever did anything to her and my boy, but they still got me in here. I *loved* them."

"I know. We all know."

Joe dragged his hands through his hair and tugged on the ends. "If y'all know it, why am I here? I can't even make funeral arrangements for them. Can't say goodbye." His breath shuddered in and out of his lungs, like he'd been on the verge of crying and his outburst had finally toppled him over the edge.

"I don't know how to tell you this. It's going to sound strange and unbelievable—impossible maybe—but I need you to understand that it's real."

"What kind of foolishness are you talking about, River?"

"Vampires. I need to tell you that vampires ex—"

"I know they do."

She blinked and stared at him through the bars. "You do?"

"I know one. Hell, I... I was involved with one."

Things clicked into place and made a morbid kind of sense to River. She moved closer to the bars and lowered her voice. "This is real important, Joe. I need you to tell me everything you can about this vampire, because it might lead us to discovering what happened to Pam and Jack. Okay? Did this vampire give you a name?"

"Emma," he whispered, then cleared his throat and said again, louder, "Her name was Emmaleigh."

River fumbled a notepad out of her purse and scribbled with a pencil. "How'd you meet her."

"I met her at Club Delirium... uh, it's a club that, uh, caters to..."

She held up her hand. "I know what they cater to. What can you tell me about your relationship with Emmaleigh?"

Joe shrugged and looked away. "Saw her at the bar and bought her a drink. Danced. Met her the next night, then the next. That's when I let her..." He gestured to his throat with one hand.

"Did you ever talk to her about Pam and Jack?"

"Not in any detail. She knew I was divorced. She listened to me, you know? But really, we didn't talk much. That's not what I wanted. Not what she wanted either. I just wanted to feel good, and she gave me that."

"How long were you with her?"

"About two years, maybe. It wasn't serious. It wasn't like..." He gulped back a thick sound in his throat and closed his eyes. "She wasn't Pam. No amount of sex could change that. About a year ago, she told me she was moving away, and I never saw her again."

"That's it?"

"Okay, it hurt. All right? It hurt a whole goddamned lot that she'd leave after staying in my place all them weeks. Out of the blue, she tells me she's on her way out of town and won't be back. She told me to make up with Pam and get my life back on track. Left me money."

"Money?"

"Yeah. It had to be from her. I found an envelope of cash in my sock drawer the day after she left."

"Did it feel genuine?"

Joe shrugged. "I guess. I was pissed a long time at her for going and didn't want to take the money at first, but it felt like a waste to trash thirty grand. Why?"

The picture he painted of Emmaleigh didn't add up with what she imagined about the vampire who took Pam and Jack.

"A vampire hurt your family. A real bad vampire. I don't know if this Emmaleigh had anything to do with it, but I'm going to find out."

His hands clenched and his cheeks mottled red. "I should have known better than to go to that damned place. I caused this to happen. Didn't I? I put them both in danger, and now it's all my fault they're dead."

"No, Joe. No… You can't know that." She tried to reach for his hands through the bars, but he jerked back and stumbled away until his back hit the far wall of the cell. "You can't blame yourself for this."

"I damned well can. Fooling around with a vampire got my family killed. Got... Dusty told me what they done to Pam. Said someone r-r—" He couldn't finish the sentence and broke into sobs, tilting his head forward toward his chest and shuddering against the wall.

River hated everything about their impossible situation, especially the warlock responsible for it. Grimly, she planned to beg the Circle of Seven to let her witness his binding and execution. She wanted to be present when they stripped him of his immortality and to see him hang. Then she could return and tell Joe how much the asshole suffered.

He deserved that.

"I'm going to get justice for Pam and Jack," she promised. "The cops know you didn't do it, but there's no safer place for you to be right now if there's a vampire out there hunting for your blood."

"Why can't I just stay home then? They can't come inside unless I invite them."

"Vampires, yeah. But whoever they're working with isn't a vampire, and they can go wherever they want. They have somebody on their side who can operate during the daylight."

Believing stone walls and metal bars could protect Joe from a warlock was foolish, but it was the best option they had. Whoever their mystery mage was, he'd have to be desperate to blast his way through a police department, even one as rural and understaffed as the Atropos PD.

Joe tugged at his hair and sank down on his narrow cot. He dropped his head between his hands. "Go on then. Go find who did this. Just keep me informed, okay? Do that much for me."

"I will."

"Tell Dusty you need my phone. I got a photo of Emma in there somewhere, and that'll at least tell you what she looks like."

"Thank you, Joe."

River unlocked his cell then made her way up front to Dusty's office. "I unlocked it so he can stretch his legs and come out if he wants to, but he understands why he's here now."

Dusty's brows raised. "And you told him about the blood drinkers?"

"Yeah… I have good news and bad news for you."

"Hit me with it. Good news first."

"Joe already knew about vampires and all this paranormal stuff."

"Okay, and the bad?"

"He was involved romantically with one until last year. Her name's Emmaleigh. I need you to try to run her name through the system and find out anything you can about her."

"A first name isn't much to go on."

"You have his cell phone, right? He said there's a picture of her. Probably all her contact info as well."

The chief pulled the phone out of the bin where they had stored Joe's personal effects. He powered it on then flipped through the contact list.

"Emmaleigh Whittaker," he read. "Have a phone number here but no address. Here's her picture."

He turned the phone around and showed a photograph of a young woman with pale blonde hair and flawless, ivory skin. Her sunny smile contradicted the image of a murderer River had expected.

"I'll see what I can dig up on her."

"Great. Thanks, Dusty. Hey, do you think you can send that picture to me?"

"Sure."

After relaying the rest of her chat with Joe, River took off and drove back toward home. Along the way, she saw Ian meandering down the sidewalk with an enormous red-furred hound. The dog wore an orange working-dog service halter.

One of his front legs was black from the elbow down, gleaming metal beneath the summer sun.

"Cool," she muttered to herself. Sometimes science impressed her as much as magic.

She drove past them without acknowledgment and pulled into the driveway a few minutes later. Joe's despair and the renewed memory of what she experienced in the recreation center killed her desire for nookie, but she could at least give Zac some affection. After locking the door, River stepped out of her shoes and flew up the stairs to their bedroom.

Back when they first made the duplex into a single-family home, they'd picked her bedroom to become their new digs because she had the better mattress and furniture. River expected to find him reading and waiting for her with a chilled bottle of wine and a bottle of massage oil to knead away the stress of the past few days.

The reality was a snoring man in an unattractive position, no wine, no book. Asleep.

Two months ago, he would have waited for her, naked in bed, reading on a tablet to pass the time. Now he slept in pajama bottoms and a T-shirt.

River frowned.

Something was happening to their relationship, and she didn't like it.

CHAPTER 8

The vampire knights didn't arrive as promised, and thanks to the tip from Joe, River had a valuable lead pointing her in the next direction.

Club Delirium.

An important meeting with a foreign software developer had pulled Zacarias to Austin. As much as he wanted to reschedule it, the plans had been in the works for months and required both him and Harrison to appear, since they were business partners. Their indie video game company, Spellbound Media, had produced a handful of popular, prosperous fantasy games.

River made the wise decision to leave him in the dark about her intentions, but she didn't dare to waltz into a vampire bar without taking some heavy-hitting backup along with her. In lieu of her werejaguar, she asked Maiara to accompany her into San Antonio. Who better to watch her back than a bear?

Club Delirium occupied a nondescript brick building in downtown San Antonio, with an underground parking garage nestled beside it. They forked over a twenty to cover their entrance fee and stepped down into a room designed like something out of a gothic horror mashed with a porno.

Crimson silk covered the walls, and all the furnishings were black edged in silver. Wall sconces designed to look like flaming torches gave the room dim lighting and an ominous atmosphere. The brightest lights were centered over five dancing poles situated in a circle in the middle of the room.

"This place reeks of desperation and blood," Maiara muttered. They made their way to the bar through a maze of round sofas and high-top tables. The early evening crowd consisted mostly of older men sipping whiskey and a few college coeds wearing black lipstick and too much eyeshadow.

"Considering what I know of the place and what Joe told me, desperation is spot on." Lots of humans eager to experience their own *Twilight* flocked to the place in droves.

"How do this many even know about it?" Maiara asked.

River shrugged. "I bet you most don't. For the majority, this is just a fetish club."

The two women settled at the bar and were eventually approached by a fair-skinned man in black slacks and a scarlet waistcoat, a neat bow tie fastened beneath the collar of his white shirt.

"What can I get you two ladies?"

Maiara's nostrils flared as she leaned forward without breaking eye contact. "We will both take bottled water for now. We're waiting for an associate."

His brows rose, but he shrugged it off and stepped away to grab two bottles.

"Blood junkie," Maiara whispered in her ear. The tough bear shifter leaned forward against the bar on both forearms, thick biceps flexing with enough muscle to snap River's neck.

He returned and set a pair of Aquafinas in front of them, the plastic damp with condensation. River ignored her drink to open the message sent from Joe's phone. "Have you seen this girl around here?"

The bartender gave the photo a brief look. "No idea. You need anything else?"

"I'd love for you to take another look," River pressed, waving the screen.

"Unless it involves pouring you a drink, I'm not interested. Got it?"

"Okay, sure," Maiara said. "Bloody Mary."

The bartender's scowl transitioned to a crooked grin. He made the drink, but when he slid it toward Maiara, she lunged for his fingers and forced his wrist to the countertop with a dull thump.

"I want the truth from you, leech-kisser. Have you seen this woman or not?"

"I'll yell for security. He'll have you both out on your asses."

"Or I could use your arms for toothpicks before security reaches us. Try me."

The man blanched. "You wouldn't. We have a truce with the San Antonio clans."

Maiara's sharp-toothed grin widened. "Not with my clan. So, talk or toothpicks? You choose. Three. Two. O—"

"Whoa, whoa. Information like that costs something, lady. I can get my ass handed to me on a silver plate if I talk. So, uh, what's it worth to ya?"

"How about I don't break your fingers one by one?" Maiara's pleasant smile contradicted the stern look in her brown eyes. She flexed one arm, and one of his fingers made a sound River didn't think fingers were supposed to make.

"Okay, okay, I'll talk. Damn. Call your twitchy muscle off already," he said to River.

"Information first," she replied. "Prove to me you know her and tell me her name."

"That's Emmaleigh. She used to be a regular around here."

Maiara applied more pressure. "Used to be?"

"Ow, ow. Fuck! I'm giving you the information, lady. Ease off of it." When the bear shifter grinned and released him, he cradled his hand against his chest and made a pitiful sound in his throat. "You didn't have to do all of that."

"Then tell us what the hell you know about her," River said.

"She bartended some nights and was a customer on others. Even picked herself up a human toy, visited him here regularly at first, and then neither of them came around for about a year. Then one day she showed up again, sans blood sack, and talked about leaving town. Said she wanted to say goodbye to everyone before she hit the road."

"Where'd she go?"

"Last I heard, she transferred up to the Boston area."

"We tried running the name Emmaleigh Whittaker through police databases and didn't turn up a thing. You have any idea why?"

"Vamps usually burn their identities after a while. You know, keeps everybody from realizing the same person has been living across the U.S. for fifty years without aging."

"So she likely changed her name."

"On her ID, at least. Most always go by the same name, but their paperwork says different."

River slid off her stool and pocketed her water bottle into her purse. She dropped a ten to cover it. "Thanks, you've been helpful."

"You won't be thanking me soon," he replied before taking the bill away with his uninjured hand.

"C'mon, let's get outta here." Maiara led the way back through the club and brushed past the lone doorman, another ghoul with a vacant look in his eyes.

A cool breeze blew down the deserted street. At some point while they were inside, the street lamps had flickered to life. The setting sun cast gold and pink streaks across the darkening sky. River frowned and picked up her pace down the sidewalk.

"I can never find the damned keys in this purse," River grumbled. She dug her hand through the small bag in search of the key ring.

A shadow flitted by them, the dark silhouette vaguely human in the dimmed garage. The lights flickered above them, and the hairs rose on her nape. Maiara paused midstride and closed one hand around River's upper arm.

"Do you sense it?" Maiara asked in a low voice.

"Yes," River whispered back.

The shifter growled, noise resonating from her in a feral snarl. "Stay behind me."

The shadows coalesced into a single form. The vampire hissed and advanced, but River didn't trust that they'd sent only one against her. A prickling feeling at the back of her neck warned her to turn around.

"They're behind us too."

Maiara exploded out of her clothes, ribbons of denim and shredded cotton flying as she expanded into the body of a massive black bear. She roared a challenge and met the first vampire in a tremendous clash.

River activated the flame ring on her finger. She didn't trust her aim with the stake she also carried, but she had magic, and more than enough of it for the pair of vampires racing across the concrete. They must have been newly born, their cheeks still pink and vibrant with the remnants of their former lives.

And too stupid to avoid the spell over her head in a fantastic arm of roaring heat. Her spell magnified it into a crackling inferno before spiraling toward the nearest vampire. It obliterated him to ashes and bone, but the second monster to his rear streaked across the lot and rolled to put out the flames.

River whirled in time to see Maiara dragging one of the vampires off his feet and slamming him onto the ground. Her claws tore away flesh and denim. She snarled and yanked, and the grisly sound of a tearing body accompanied his agonized scream. The second vampire assailant punched her in the side, and if it hurt the bear shifter, it did nothing to halt her attack. She yanked a limb off the vampire beneath her, like a child pulling wings from a fly.

Reaching deep and allowing magic from her bangles to pool at the tips of her fingers, River thrust out and directed a rush of kinetic force to slam the second bloodsucker away.

Blowing him off did nothing. More emerged from the shadows of the parking garage. They rushed in blurs of color, some on two legs and others on four, leaping and crossing ground faster than River could count them.

Was it five, or six?

Maiara left the mauled vampire on the ground and charged toward the group, but she was outnumbered. They leapt on her, biting and clawing at her furred back.

River drew on her power and struck out with force, fueled by her desperate desire to survive. The nearest vampire stopped short, as if he had slammed against an invisible wall. Then he toppled back to the dirty pavement. Another rushed in from the side and plowed into her before she had a chance to strike. They hit the ground together and rolled, his teeth gnashing inches from her face as she tried to fend him off by burying her fingernails into his cheeks.

She lost sight of her companion in the scuffle, but she heard Maiara's growling roar. The sound echoed across the garage. Clutching the stake so hard she felt her pulse thumping in her fingers, she blindly plunged it upward.

And missed.

Not that it mattered that she'd missed the creature's heart. It abandoned the attack, leaping off her, driven away either by pain or fear of getting ashed.

Scrambling to her feet, River ignited the flame ring again and released another flaming projectile. But she could only fire in one direction and the vampires had her surrounded. Maiara's pelt glistened with blood, and it was only a matter of time until the werebear fell beneath the onslaught.

As another vampire hurtled across the pavement, Maiara lunged forward and intercepted it. They crashed together, snarling, only for her to haul the bloodsucker beneath her massive claws. She slammed it once, twice, and then it was dusty bones and ash beneath her.

More fledglings emerged from the shadows, a veritable army of cannon fodder. There were too many for them to fight.

River clapped her hands out in front of her and rubbed her palms together, channeling every ounce of focus she possessed into the only spell she thought could get them out of this. Her hands shook and her pulse spiked with the effort, but a spark flared between her fingertips.

Golden radiance flashed over the parking garage, flooding the darkened space with sunlight. Although River only held the spell for a second, it vaporized the closest vampires and those furthest from it shrieked out in pain, their wails an ear-splitting cacophony in the returning darkness.

Overcome by the surge of her own power, River swayed on her feet and stumbled forward against the nearest car, clutching at the side-view mirror to remain upright. Her legs wobbled and her knees gave out, pitching her down to the floor.

CHAPTER 9

Zacarias was ten minutes away from home when the call reached him from Maiara. He pressed the pedal to the floor, blazing the rest of the way into town and even passing an APD officer dozing in his patrol vehicle. Either they'd been tipped off by Dusty to leave the shifter crew alone, or he decided sleeping was a better use of his time than chasing a Jag.

He slowed once he reached the residential streets and turned onto their lane. Maiara waited for him on the porch, hair free around the shoulders of a shirt stolen from his closet.

"Where is she?"

"Right here in your living room. There was an attack in the parking garage beside the Delirium," the werebear explained as Zac followed on her heels.

His attention snapped to River's still form on the couch. Once he moved to her and knelt beside the sofa, he took her motionless hand between both of his palms, stroking over the back of her knuckles and watching her face.

"Start at the beginning, and tell me everything."

It took her less than a minute to relay the information she and River gained from the barkeep at Club Delirium. He nodded when she described the ghoul's reluctance to divest any details. Typical.

"Then what happened?"

"An ambush. We were nearly to her car when the first of them arrived. Then there were many more. Too many, I think."

"What do you mean?"

"Covens, as far as I am aware, do not usually have so many fledglings among their number. None of the dozen or two who came against us were well trained or powerful, but their numbers gave them the advantage."

"How the hell did you get out of it?"

"She summoned sunlight," she said. "It saved our lives, but she collapsed afterward, and I drove us back."

"Were you followed?"

"Would we be here if we were?"

"Good point," he grumbled. "Thank you for getting her home safely."

Maiara waved his apology off. "Will she be all right?"

"Yeah, she just needs to rest. The spell must have overtaxed her." He brushed a curl back from River's face, then twisted around to look at the other shifter. "What about you? Were you hurt?"

"Nothing I can't recover from. These bites will sting like a bitch for a while, but you know how it is."

After drawing an afghan over River, he left her on the sofa and led Maiara into their kitchen to introduce her to the pots and containers of leftover food waiting in the fridge. He'd cooked three times that week, and they'd barely had enough time to enjoy any of it.

"Help yourself to whatever you need, and I'll, uh—" He glanced at her shirt. "I'll get you some jeans that fit too."

Before Zac could take a step away, his phone rang with an incoming call, the name Ian MacArthur flashing across the touch screen. He answered and raised it to his ear. "Ian, this isn't a great time."

"Lyle and I have a lead. A fresh vamp trail in the area. You might want to get in on this because the two knights from Rosenhaven haven't checked in with us yet. What's the news on the girls?"

The hairs on Zac's arms rose, frost gliding down his nape. "Maiara and River were attacked while checking out a local vampire fetish club in San Antonio."

Ian sucked in his breath. "Shit. How are they? Any injuries?"

"River overextended herself casting magic, and Maiara's healing."

"If you need to stay with her, we'll wait on backup from the others."

Zac glanced toward the living room at River's peaceful form, steady breaths raising and lowering her chest in the easy rhythm of sleep.

Maiara touched his arm. "You go and provide help to them. I'll stay here and keep watch over your woman." She crossed her arms, strong biceps bulging impressively despite a newly healed, pink line running from wrist to elbow on one arm.

"Thanks, Maiara. Look, the thresholds here are probably strong enough to incinerate a vampire master, plus there's wards on every door and window to boot. Just keep her comfy. Tell her where I am if she wakes up while I'm gone."

"No problem."

"Glad that's settled," Ian said. "Meet us at the playground on the corner of Smith and Abigail."

Five minutes later, Zac pulled up to the curb alongside a playground in an older neighborhood. Ian stood beneath a lamppost with Lyle sitting at his feet.

"Here?"

"This is where Lyle picked up on the scent. Figured we should have backup following this one. Tommy is making his way on furry feet and said he'd catch up to us."

"Right. Lead the way then."

Lyle rose and shook out his coat, flapping his long ears. At any other time, it would have been comical, but the day's strenuous events drained the humor out of it.

The hound led them from the park to a mobile home community nearby, its cramped space littered with RVs and dilapidated trailers. They approached a shabby trailer with a pair of beaten-down sedans in the drive and a rusty van parked by the curb. Ice-cold panic washed over Zacarias before his heart thumped into overdrive, slamming against his chest.

"This can't be right. That's Bobby's place."

As dread dropped a leaden weight into his stomach, Zac pushed past Ian and jogged up the rickety wooden steps to the front door. His fist pounded against the peeling frame.

"Bobby? Bobby, it's Zac. You home, man?"

The door creaked open, framing a thin man with square glasses perched on the end of his nose. "Hey, Zac, what's up, man?"

"Sup, Greg. Is Bobby home?"

"He's in bed, dude. Been down all day after getting locked out on the porch last night. Guess he was too damn drunk to ring the doorbell 'cause we found him crashed out on the rocker."

"You mind if we come in? I brought a friend along who was supposed to meet Bobby over some work-related stuff, but maybe I can do a pharmacy run for him too."

"Yeah, sure. Oh, hey, cool dog. I had one like him when I was growing up."

Zac made quick introductions as Greg let them inside. Bobby shared the cramped three-bedroom trailer with two other university students. They split the costs and, judging by the leftovers on their counters, lived off a diet of pizza, ramen, and peanut butter crackers.

Lyle nosed Greg's leg in passing on the way into the single-wide trailer but otherwise ignored him. He strained against his leash and pulled Ian to the closed door leading to Bobby's room.

Zac steeled himself, opened the door, and stepped inside with Ian and Lyle close on his heels. "Hey, man, you okay?"

Bobby shivered beneath his blankets and pulled them tighter around himself. "I feel like crap, dude. Can't keep anything down."

"Yeah, that happens when you're sick. You should have called. River could have cooked something up for ya."

The room smelled like honeysuckle with an underlying stale odor, like old meat approaching expiration. Zac glanced around and flipped the light switch on to chase away the shadows. Then he crouched to look under the bed. Nothing was there except empty soda cans and a pair of muddy sneakers.

"Lost my damn cell phone. Why are you all up in my stuff?"

"Just having a look around." Zac opened the closet and peered in. Suits hung on hangers with scrubs and a lab coat above piles of clothes in trash bags on the floor. No lurking vampire.

Lyle growled deep in his chest then whined. With the door shut behind them, he shifted. "It's him. Your friend is the vampire."

Bobby groaned from beneath the blanket. "I'm too tired to even be startled by what just happened. Ugh. Why is there a naked dog-man in my room?"

Zac groaned into one of his hands and leaned against the wall, running his fingers up into his hair. "Fuck. What do we do, Ian?"

"What's going on? Why's everyone so serious? Why's this naked dude here? Goddammit, tell me something."

"Normally, I'd advise you to phone Rosenhaven for help, but given the circumstances…" Ian frowned. "I may have a place for him. I need to make some calls. In the meantime, we can't leave him here. Another day or two and his roomies will start looking like a meal."

"What's he talking about, Zac?"

Zacarias sat on the edge of the bed and dropped his hand to Bobby's blanketed shoulder. "Hey, you know I'd never lie to you about serious shit, right?"

"You're kinda scaring me, dude. What's wrong with me?"

Zac glanced at the prominent tips of his friend's canine teeth. "This isn't any kind of normal illness. You're going through a change, and in a couple days, you're going to be thirsty for any blood you can get."

Bobby's mouth fell open and his eyes widened. "You're shitting me."

"Would I shit you about something like this? What happened the night you got locked out?"

"I dunno. I went to that concert in San Antonio with Patrick last night and got back late. I was tired as all hell too. Couldn't find my keys, and…"

"And?"

"I dunno. I must have sat down and passed out. Next thing I remember was Greg kicking me awake this morning and feeling hungover all day long. I… You think I'm a vampire? Really?"

"Really," Zac said in a quiet voice.

"I can't be a vampire. No way. Doesn't that mean someone sucked my blood and I...?"

"Drank theirs in return?" Ian supplied. "It does. Your blackout sounds a little too convenient. Like you'd been bewitched."

"I can't be a vampire. I'm beginning my residency this fall." His voice rose and cracked as the reality set in, panic filling his widening eyes and terror in his ashen features.

"Hate to break it to you, pal, but that ain't gonna happen." Zac sat on the edge of the bed and laid his hand on Bobby's shoulder. "This isn't a joke, and it sure as hell won't be easy, but we're going to help you any way we can."

"Doesn't this mean I'm *dead?*"

"No, it's not like the movies. Think of it more like... a disease. A disease that makes you a little more..." Zac struggled to find the silver lining in the bleak, sunless clouds that had claimed Bobby's life.

"Faster and stronger," Lyle suddenly cut in, catching on to their desperate attempts to remain upbeat for Bobby's sake. "You won't ever get sick again. Ain't that right, Ian?"

"Right," Ian said. "You won't begin your residency this fall, but I can promise you'll complete it in time once you've mastered control of your hunger for blood."

Although he was already pale for his usual chestnut brown complexion, Bobby turned a sickly shade of slate gray. "Blood, oh fuck no. But I have to—I mean I can't eat—" He gulped and twisted around on his bed, then dry heaved into the trash bin sitting nearby.

"At least you won't have to live on ramen anymore. That's always a plus," Ian muttered.

"How can you guys be so calm about all this?"

Zac swallowed the hard lump in his throat. "Because we have to be."

Greg rapped on the door. "Hey. Everything okay in there?"

Lyle glanced over his shoulder then popped into his dog form again. Zac opened the door.

"Hey, I'm going to bring Bobby to urgent care and then to my place so River can fuss over him," Zac said.

"Oh cool. Thanks, I guess." Greg lowered his voice. "To be honest, we were all kind of worried he'd spread his shit to us. I knew he'd pick up something doing all of that volunteering last week."

"Yeah, he's looking pretty ragged. I'll give you a call once he's seen someone, okay?"

"Sure. You feel better, man, okay?" Greg peered around Zac before disappearing down the hall.

With Ian's help, Zac got Bobby out of bed and out to his van. He only hoped inviting a fledgling vampire into their house wouldn't bite him in the ass later. Or other places.

***

The stench of vampire worsened by the hour as Bobby underwent transition from human to immortal blood drinker. Zac kept watch over him until he dozed and blinked his eyes open to find his pal hungrily eyeballing his jugular, they decided not to take chances with Bobby's safety or their own.

By that time, he'd began to feel the hunger and voluntarily allowed them to restrain him to the headboard.

"Don't wanna hurt y'all. I can't describe it, but I don't feel like me anymore."

"You're still the same you, Bobby."

"Aside from never seeing the sun again, right?"

"Actually, no. A lot of vampires have homes with special glass, and they do the same with their car windows."

"But I won't be able to go outside. No afternoon dates or hanging with you guys down at Fiesta Texas or Moody Gardens."

"Hey, there's always winter. Sun sets at 6:00 p.m. and then it's on, bro." Bobby appeared unconvinced, but Zac quickly continued on to the subject of food, deciding to break the news clean and quick. Like ripping off a Band-Aid. "Anyway, Tommy went to grab you something to eat. You'll feel better once you get a sip."

Bobby blanched. "What do you mean?"

"A deer or boar or something."

"No way. I can't bite an animal's neck."

"Look, if we gotta put it in a cup for you, we will, but it's gonna taste the same way going down," Zac said.

"Ugh. I'll try the cup, okay? Pretty sure Riv would be pissed if you dragged a dead animal up here onto her guest bed."

The first smile of the evening broke across Zac's face, short-lived but amused nonetheless. "Yeah, you're probably right."

"How is she, anyway?"

"She didn't even move when I put her in bed."

"She gonna be okay?"

Zac drew in a deep breath. "Yeah. Yeah, she will." He couldn't think about the alternative, and it was easier to pretend everything was fine than to wring his hands and pace their bedroom. "Get some rest. I'll be back up with your drink soon."

"Thanks."

Zac wandered downstairs again. Ian, Lyle, and Maiara all sat around his dining room table in deep discussion about the evening's events.

"There were too many in place so soon after sunset for it not to have been planned. They knew we would be there," Maiara said.

Ian set his phone on the table. "But how? That's the big question. How did they know to expect you?"

"Never mind that for now. What are we going to do about Bobby?" Zac asked.

Ian glanced up from his cup of coffee. The guy lived on it, chugging one cup after the next since they'd returned three hours ago with the vampire in their care. Zac assumed it was a military officer thing and kept the pot full. "Arrangements have been made. I'll drive Bobby to Houston this afternoon once we've all had some sleep. Your friend isn't changed enough yet for sunlight to kill him. Those few hours will give us a head start out of the area."

"Then what happens to him?"

Ian shrugged. "Avery and her small brood will teach him what he needs to know to survive for the rest of his immortal life. More importantly, they'll keep him out of sight and out of Rosenhaven's hands. My acquaintance has connections in Louisiana, so they can always head there if things in Texas get too messy."

"How long? I mean, when will we see him again?"

"Most small covens aren't willing to take in stray vampires they're not responsible for turning. We lucked out. Avery owed me a favor. It could be a couple years before he's safe around humans and has his thirst under control."

"Why Bobby? I mean, what the hell did they have to gain from biting and leaving him like that?"

Lyle stroked his chin and leaned back in his seat, a beer bottle propped on his thigh. "I think turning your friend was a way to get to you."

"But how?"

"Think about it. If I learned anything in prison and from the time I was working with my old boss, it's that you go through somebody's friends and loved ones if you wanna hurt them," he replied.

From what Zac had gathered, the dog shifter used to be a gang enforcer for some big drug dealer out in East Texas. Whatever his past, Ian trusted him, which meant Tommy and Argus had also placed their faith in him. That was enough for Zac.

"Then we should get the rest of the guys and either tell them to get the hell out of town or come and stay here."

"Good idea." Ian nodded. "Hunker down here after sunset, work by day. A normal human with a concealed carry can handle a ghoul if there's any in the area, and most of them aren't that damned bold yet."

"Patrick carries, and he's surrounded by hard pipe-hitting dudes all day," Zac said with a grin. "I'm not too worried about him until dark, but I'll pass the word along."

"Did you just quote *Pulp Fiction* at us?" Lyle asked.

Zac chuckled. "Maybe. Anyway, I'm not too worried about him. They can handle themselves against any ghoul until nightfall, and after that, they can rely on thresholds and private property to keep any bloodsuckers away."

"What's your pal do?"

"He's in a garage band, but he's in good with a local motorcycle club filled with members who know how to get things done, if you get my drift."

"Ah. Gotcha." Lyle's grin widened. "The right type in this situation."

It took less than a couple hours to make the necessary phone calls to his friends, beginning with Harrison, since his close pal would help him spread the word around the community.

"You want everyone notified? You got it, bro."

There was no one more committed to sharing the news than a raven shifter. After ending the call, Zacarias phoned Darrell.

"Hey, dude. Were you asleep?"

The voice on the other end of the line hesitated a moment before releasing a long yawn. "Yeah. *Was* is the operative word here. What's up?"

"Sorry. You know I wouldn't call unless it was an emergency."

"Something else happen?"

"River was attacked down in San Antonio. She's not hurt, but the shit is gonna hit the fan any day now. Dozens of vampires came after her and this other shifter helping us out. On top of that... Bobby is a vampire now. They got to him."

The line went silent save for the sound of Darrell's heavy breaths. A long pause stretched over several heart beats until at last his friend replied with a soft spoken, "For real?"

"Yeah, so please, do me a favor and stay indoors after sunset. Don't open the door for anyone you don't recognize, and if you do recognize them, do *not* invite them inside. Let them walk in of their own accord if they're capable of passing a threshold."

"All right. Fuck. Yeah, I can do that. Thanks for letting me know, and tell Bobby I'm... shit. What do you even say in a situation like this?"

"I don't know either. He's pretty depressed, and I can't blame him."

"What's going to happen to him now?"

"We have a friend who will look after him. Anyway, tomorrow night, all of you are welcome to bunk here until this shit is settled."

Darrell didn't provide an immediate response, but Zac released a long, pent-up breath when his pal finally replied with, "I'll be over before sunset then. This shit is scary enough, and sitting here alone at my place doesn't help."

"Thanks. See you tomorrow. Err, tonight."

Zac ended the call and phoned Patrick next. The conversation went the same, awakening both his pal and the poor guy's girlfriend. Like Darrell, he swore over the unfortunate news of Bobby's transformation.

"That fucking sucks, man. No more sunlight?"

"No more sunlight. Permanent liquid diet in his future. Well, I guess some bloodsuckers do like solid food, but… anyway. I don't want this to happen to you guys too. If you and Jessie have plans to vacation out of town or want to come over here, you're welcome to join us."

"Man, are you kidding me? No way I want her knowing about this shit."

"Then take a trip. I hear Orlando's nice this time of year."

"Yeah, we can do that. I've been saving up."

Zac hung up after relaying the same warnings about thresholds and invitations. His friends were smart enough to heed them. With that done, he rang the police chief and caught Dusty up on the news.

"Go get some sleep," Ian advised after Zac hung up the phone for the last time.

"But River—"

"Will appreciate if you don't run yourself ragged," the older man said in his sensible, matter-of-fact tone. "There isn't anything else we can do right now. It's their time, and if they are lurking out there awaiting the chance to strike, they'll be disappointed. This threshold is solid."

"Point made." Zac rubbed his face with both hands and groaned into his palms. "I'm just so worried about her, dude. I don't know if I can sleep."

Ian placed an arm around his shoulder and led him toward the stairs. "Then just lie beside your woman and be there for her."

CHAPTER 10

River awakened with a splitting headache to find Zacarias passed out beside her in boxers and the shirt he'd worn the previous day. Her bladder screamed for relief, and her stuffy head felt like someone had taken a chisel to it.

Her boyfriend didn't stir when she crawled from beside him. Sensing he needed the rest, she left him undisturbed and crept away to pee in the adjacent bathroom. When she emerged after washing her hands and stepped into the quiet hallway, the disturbing sensation of icy fingers ran down the middle of her spine, tracing her back and raising the fine hairs of her nape and arms.

Something's in the house!

With her witch's sixth sense engaged, River flew into action and rushed from room to room of the upper floor until she found the source of the discomfort.

Bobby's corpse lay in the guest bed with disheveled sheets and a thin blanket around his middle. His head tilted back against the pillow, cheeks sunken and gaunt, dry lips parted.

They were keeping a dead man inside her house.

Terror slammed her heart against her ribs and a shriek tore from her lungs. Stumbling back, she slammed against the wall behind her and banged one hip on the door jamb, no doubt creating a nasty bruise. Something, perhaps whatever entity she felt in her home, had killed Bobby.

Heart still galloping a hundred miles a minute, she gasped when her gaze fell to the pointed vampire teeth shining ivory against Bobby's cracked lower lip.

"What's wrong?" Zac called. "River? Where are you?"

Footsteps thundered up the stairs and from the bedroom, shifters flooding into the guest room from every area of the home in varying states of undress. Ian was the only one in pants between the three of them, Maiara clothed in boy shorts and a camisole, Lyle in only his boxers.

Before she could dart away, Zac surrounded her with both of his arms. "River, baby, it's all right."

"Why is Bobby a vampire? Why is he in our guest room? What happened?"

"A lot," Zac said grimly.

"We were in the garage at Delirium and there were vampires everywhere. Now our friend is a vampire, and I *sensed* him and knew he was here before I even came in the room," she blurted out.

"Yeah, and Maiara got you out of there after you passed out. You've been unconscious for hours."

She glanced at Maiara. The stoic bear shifter nodded.

"I'll put on some coffee," Ian said.

"I'm going back to bed," Lyle muttered before he shambled off.

Despite all the commotion in the room, Bobby didn't stir. He made a single, rasping breath, as if choking for air, then resumed the soundless and even rhythm.

"I'll explain everything, I promise," Zac said as he guided her down the stairs.

Between the three of them, Zac, Maiara, and Ian caught River up to date on the events she'd missed since passing out.

"Have you ever cast a spell like that before?" Ian asked.

"No. To be honest, I didn't even realize I could do it until then." While gazing down at her cupped palms, she tried to envision the same flicker of sunlight glowing warm and radiant over her hands. The lingering headache throbbed in warning as golden light spilled down to her fingertips, flickered, and died within seconds of the summoning.

Maiara leaned forward, resting an elbow on the table to study her. "Yes. Like that, only much larger than any spell I ever witnessed. It was truly magnificent, as if you had turned the night into day," she said. "The closest vampires turned to dust and everyone at the edges of the spell retreated."

Casting the spell so soon after depleting her energy stores made her want to vomit. Bile rose in her throat, but she washed the sour taste from her mouth with a swig of hot coffee. "I don't think I can do it again like that."

As far as she knew, there wasn't a witch alive capable of casting a spell without a focus item or totem of some kind. They crafted enchanted objects, worked in natural remedies, and brewed potions. Witches, whether male or female, used the world around them and nature itself to create magic. Magicians, on the other hand, were born of magic itself, and they were *always* male. What she had done—creating a magical spell from her own life energy— had been the act of a junior wizard.

"Like I said, you've been passed out for hours. Don't push yourself." Zac leaned over and kissed her brow.

"I won't. What's the next step?" she asked.

"Darrell is going to come here. Safety in numbers and all that. Plus, we don't want to end up with more vampire pals, right?"

"Right." She thought about poor Bobby upstairs and closed her eyes. Someone had stolen his life from him and irrevocably changed the course of his entire future. "I feel so bad for him."

Ian grimaced. "As do I. But you have my word I'll do everything I can to support the transition to his new life. I have contacts on the board at the University of Texas. Arrangements can be made regarding his education once it's safe for him to return." He gazed out the window, eyes narrowed in thought. "Evening clinicals. Perhaps we'll donate new windows to the medical facilities in the area."

While Zacarias and Ian discussed ways to make life easier for Bobby in his future as a vampire, River excused herself from the table and located her phone.

She called Pythia, dreading her mentor's reaction to the news and also wondering why the hell no one had contacted her for updates. She'd dealt with the group of older witches breathing down her neck for lesser issues in the past.

"Pythia speaking," her friend announced over the phone.

"Hey, I'm checking in, and boy do we have some problems here. You won't believe what happened."

"Should I take a Xanax first before you tell me?" Pythia asked, voice dry. "Let's have it."

By the time River had completed her story of the past days' events, her friend's silence made her lower the phone and check the screen to confirm the phone hadn't powered off.

"That's quite an accomplishment. You created sunlight from nothing, like a magician?"

"From nothing, and then I spent the rest of the night passed out in bed. Tell me this is enough reason to go after Rosenhaven. They obviously orchestrated the entire assault and tried to have me killed because I was too close."

Pythia quieted again.

"Well?"

"It isn't as easy as siccing every witch in the region on this one vampire coven, River."

"Why not? They *attacked* me."

"Do you have any proof they were behind it? Did you see Margot Calloway or another master vampire pulling the strings?"

"No, but—"

"Allow me to confer with the Trinity." The line went silent while River twirled the length of her charger cable around her finger. Her mentor returned moments later. "At this point in time, we remain unable to take action without initiating a war between our side and the vampires."

"If we don't, the shifters will, Pythia. We have to do something, otherwise—"

"Then if there is to be war, let it be on the heads of the shifters. The Daughters of the Moon will take no part in it, and that includes you. We can't afford to participate in their vendetta against the Children of the Night. We would lose countless witches joining this senseless feud between the shapeshifters and vampires. Good witches who have no formal combat training or ability to defend themselves."

River lowered the phone and stared at the glowing screen, as if that would change Pythia's verdict. She'd never heard her friend give a decree in such a taciturn matter, or with so much finality.

"Pythia—"

"You heard what I said. You've only proven there are dangerous vampires in the area and done nothing to tie the incident to Rosenhaven. Unless you have irrefutable evidence to the contrary, I declare the matter to be closed."

"And what about the Blood Sacrament? The vampires are only involved because a warlock brought them into it."

"Then I suggest you find the warlock who cast the spell. I'm sorry, River, but our hands are tied."

"Then can you at least send someone to help me? This is huge. Well beyond the standard assessments."

"Should I report back to the Circle of Seven that you can't fulfill the task?"

"I never said that!" With River's outburst, the ceiling lights flickered and buzzed, creating feedback. "You don't understand. If you don't believe me, come back to Atropos and breathe in the air. Look at the sky and feel how the earth trembles under your feet. Something is wrong here, and if you don't convince the Three to send help, more than shifters are going to suffer. Lots of humans are going to *die*."

"I'm not in Texas."

Furious, River hung up the phone and spun through her contacts log. She called a witch on the west coast, and after thirty minutes of receiving the runaround, was directed to a stern grandmother who told her to calm down, smoke a joint, and relax.

"What the hell?" River demanded after ending the call. She'd been summarily chastised for trying to go above Pythia's head and told to chill out, all in the same sentence.

And with each call she made afterward, the authority on the end echoed the same sentiment.

River was on her own.

***

Steam billowed up from the liquid boiling in the cauldron. River pursed her lips and inhaled the aroma while studying the yellow-green contents. The color wasn't right, but she'd followed the instructions down to the letter.

Maybe following the instructions was where she'd gone wrong. Considering that, she pushed the book aside and returned to the cabinets. Jars clinked together as she sifted through her varied collection and pulled several down to the counter. She took a pinch of the herbs in one and a single dried leaf from another, then crushed them together in her mortar.

An overwhelming sense of intuition guided her, urging River to sprinkle the ground herbs into the cauldron while stirring the contents in a clockwise direction. The color faded translucent, clear as water with only a few shimmering motes of energy hanging suspended in the solution.

She'd created the perfect energy-absorbing potion. She moved the cauldron to a trivet at the window and pulled up the blinds. Sunlight spilled in, halfway blinding her after so long in the dimly lit room. Exhausted, River plopped down in a chair to rest her aching back. She preferred to brew on her feet and had been standing for hours.

"Safe to come in?" Zac called from behind her.

"Oh, yeah." She twisted in her seat and waved him in.

"Whatcha making?"

"If I get this right, sunshine in a bottle. I'm hoping to make enough to pass out to everyone in the event of an emergency."

Zac rubbed his palms over his eyes and yawned as he took the seat beside her. "Sounds good. Makes you wonder, though, where they're getting so much corpsefodder."

She didn't bother correcting him, since everyone knew vampires weren't dead. "Why don't you go back to bed?" she asked. "Ian said you were awake all night keeping an eye on me."

"Nah, I'm good. I'd hoped to be up before he left with Bobby, but I guess that didn't happen."

"You needed the sleep, so we didn't wake you. Besides, Bobby wasn't entirely awake, himself. Ian wasn't too worried about becoming a snack for him, and I have the feeling he can handle himself if push comes to shove."

"Yeah." His gaze dropped to his lap and his shoulders slumped. "Still, I feel like I failed him."

Abandoning her potion, River moved over and slid into his lap. "Of course you didn't. No one saw this coming. *No one.* What matters now is he's in good hands. He's safe."

Zac's arms wrapped around her waist. "I know he's safe, but it doesn't exactly make me feel better. Patrick is going to take a trip out of town with his girlfriend. Darrell plans to be here before dark."

"Good. I'll put fresh sheets on the bed." If she didn't toss the mattress over the balcony rail and sacrifice it altogether. Vampires weren't exactly fragrant when undergoing the change. Bobby's body hadn't died, per se, but his changing metabolism had caused all manner of gross adjustments to occur to his body. She shuddered.

Zac squeezed her close, perceptive of how much she needed his embrace. She hugged him back in return and nuzzled her cheek against his throat before leaning back to gaze at him with all the love and warmth she could muster.

How could she possibly do this without him?

"I'm sorry," she whispered.

"Sorry for what?"

"Having to always be in the thick of every supernatural occurrence in Atropos. We're supposed to be planning that trip to Brazil and everything, and instead, we're here battling vampires and warlocks."

Zacarias lifted her off his lap and into her seat again before he rose. "Nah, it's fine. Part of living with a witch, I guess. While you handle your alchemy stuff, I'm gonna go have a word at the station."

Disappointment stabbed like a knife, chased by gut-wrenching guilt. She hadn't been a good girlfriend of late, so focused on the job that she'd neglected Zacarias. She sighed and ran her fingers through her thick curls then glanced out the window, watching until his sporty Jag zipped by.

Was this going to be their life? Did she have to pick being a witch over having a husband and a family? It made her wonder if that's why Pythia had never married, because of the responsibilities.

In fact, every single witch she knew, with exception to the mother who'd birthed her, had lived a childless, unmarried life.

"Not me," she muttered to the empty room. "I won't let that happen to me."

CHAPTER 11

I rate with Rosenhaven's failure to provide assistance as promised, River got on the phone and rang Master Tremaine again.

"My apologies, Miss Jackson," Tremaine said, voice smoother than silk. "A miscommunication and some crossed wires led to our two preferred knights initiating an investigation in the Atropos area without announcing their arrivals. They'll be there to speak with you once darkness falls. Were we able to procure the services of an Overseer, we would provide one to investigate this unapproved initiation. Unfortunately, none are in the area."

"I appreciate it." River ended the call and turned to find a pair of expectant green eyes resting on her.

"Well?" Zac asked.

"Weren't you listening?"

"I don't eavesdrop on your calls."

Exasperated, she moved close enough to swat his chest, but he caught her by the wrist and yanked her close against him, wrapping both arms around River's waist. "We'll have an extra pair of guests this evening."

"We don't have to invite them inside, do we?"

"No." She had no intention of allowing any vampire in their home. "I know we didn't want them here before, but on the off chance the coven is innocent, it's not bad to see what their people turn up. They'll gather what information we've already collected then make their way out into the town for an investigation of their own, primarily into the attack on Bobby. It's a blatant disregard for the rules. These days, no one turns a human without that mortal's permission and the approval of the local lord or lady."

Zac laced his fingers together at the small of her back. "Like that bitch would tell us if she did approve it," he muttered. "I don't like how she treated us."

A soft snort escaped before she could rein it in. "True enough. But if she was the one behind it, that'd be way too obvious, right? Plus, *their* council would have her ass for it. What would she have to gain by working with our warlock?"

"Chaos?" he asked.

"Maybe, but if Bobby had gone on a killing spree, the vampire council would have sent in an Overseer. Margot wouldn't want that."

"Overseer?"

"Think Judge Dredd, but the vampire edition. They deal out pain to rogue vamps and ask questions later usually. At least, that's how Mom explained it to me."

"Ohhh... gotcha. Okay. So, by the way, has your mom said anything about this? She tried to get you that audience with Felicity, after all, so she's got to be aware something is going on here."

The corners of her mouth tugged down. "She was on her way to take a cruise with her boyfriend, so I haven't been able to get ahold of her. It's weird, too, because she said call if I needed anything, and now I can't reach her." And now the worries returned full force, concerned about her mother's well-being. She scrunched her nose up and imagined the worst-case scenario.

"I've been on a cruise before. Phone reception is spotty at best," he reassured her. "Leave a voicemail message or a text, and she'll probably get with you as soon as she reaches an area with reception." Standing close against Zac reminded her of the intimacy lost between them recently, all plans to take their own vacation shoved aside for the foreseeable future.

She hugged him tighter. "Thank you."

"You don't need to thank me so much."

"I do. I promise, as soon as we have this all sorted and everyone's lives are back to normal, we'll head right to Brazil. No waiting for deals or a sale. I'll let you buy everything, and we'll just fly down."

A hint of a smile came to his face. She hadn't seen one in so long—a genuine one, not forced for her peace of mind—that she rose to her tiptoes and kissed him.

The chime of the doorbell interrupted, followed by a characteristic knock.

"Ugh, it's Darrell," Zac groaned as they broke apart. "Is it awful that sex is on my mind when there's angry vampires prowling around?"

No matter how much she wanted to judge him for having his mind on his piece, she couldn't, because the same thoughts had danced through her mind. No matter what happened in Atropos, they'd never been so preoccupied with her duties that they couldn't make time for each other. "No," she answered. "Go on, we'll pick this up when everyone goes to sleep."

They split up downstairs. While Zac went to let Darrell in, River joined Maiara on the couch. The bear shifter had been passing her free time by reading through River's vast collection of indie paperback romance novels.

"So, we throwing a party tonight or what?" Darrell asked. He stepped inside and grinned at them while tossing his black dreads back from his dark face. "Where's Trick?"

"He's taking Jessie to Universal. Said all the people here would cramp his style and that he'd rather spend the money giving his girl a tour of Harry Potter World instead," Zac said. He shrugged. "I can't say I blame him. Right now, I'd rather deal with fictional magical universes than the real thing."

"I think we would all prefer to be dealing with fictional magic right now," Maiara muttered as she waved the paranormal romance novel in her hand.

***

Zac waited near the front door with a coffee mug in hand and stared out through the narrow window. Streaks of gold stretched across the sky. Less than an hour from now, the sun would be gone and the vampires would arrive. The idea made his skin crawl.

"Everything all right?" River stepped up behind him and slipped her arms around his waist. She pressed up against his back and held him tight.

"Waiting for Lyle to get back." He settled a hand over her wrist and stroked his thumb across the soft skin below one of her magic bangles. She always had at least a couple on each wrist, pre-enchanted with numerous defensive spells. "He can hold his own, but we all agreed to be back before nightfall. I know the vamps are supposed to be helping, but…"

"You don't trust them."

"Yeah." He squeezed her arm then gently pulled her grip loose. Turning, he looked down at her. "I don't."

"Me either."

"Glad we're on the same page."

A sharp bark and a ferocious snarl startled Zac away from the door just about the time he was beginning to consider hopping into his Jag and tracking their pal down. Every time it seemed he and River would get a quiet moment to talk, something always came up. At least this time, he'd been expecting the interruption.

"What the hell?" Zac muttered as Lyle's noisy hound dog baying raised the hairs on his nape. It worked like a werewolf's howl, its effectiveness startling him.

"Why's that dog losing his shit outside?" Darrell asked, alarmed. He leaned forward from the seat he'd taken beside Maiara on the couch. His failed attempts of the past hour to get her phone number hadn't discouraged him from joining her and River on the sofa. A recent comedy adventure played on the television, a magical film produced by the dragon shifter, Saul Drakenstone's, company.

The moment Zac opened the door, the ginger hound barged in with his nose to the floor and his hackles raised. His wild eyes and terrifying appearance startled Maiara to her feet. She crossed the room to join them.

"Dude, what's up? Slow down a minute and tell us what's happening," Zac said.

Without shame or modesty, Lyle popped into his human body, the shift transforming even the black metal of the prosthetic limb on his left forearm. Zac never tired of watching it, awestruck by the science.

Lyle's brown eyes darted over the foyer, past Zac and River, and through the open arch leading into the living room. "The warlock is here."

"Wait, what?" Zac spun toward the door.

"No, he's inside," Lyle said. "I kept finding whiffs of his scent throughout town, man. I've been running back and forth from parking lot to lot hunting this fucker down. Then I remembered you asked me to come back before nightfall. Caught his scent in the driveway. He walked through your front door."

"Nobody but Ian, Bobby, and Darrell have passed through this front door all day, man."

Lyle stared into the living room as Darrell rose from his seat.

"It doesn't sound like your place is any safer, if that warlock entered your house at some point today, man. Anyway, thanks for the offer, but I think I'll follow Patrick's example and have a vacation out of town."

The dog shifter snarled and dove forward from two legs onto four. He landed with the next bound onto Darrell's chest, knocking Zac's friend onto his back.

"Get this crazy dude off me," Darrell cried out. He shoved at Lyle's face, but the quicker shifter snapped and aggressively growled.

Before Zac could cross the room and pull the hound off, Maiara closed her arms around his waist and drew him back. "Ian said Lyle has the best nose in all of Texas," she said.

"But that's my friend."

"Be that as it may, your friend has some questions to answer before we can allow him to go. River?"

River had frozen between the foyer and the living room, standing in the threshold of the open archway separating the two areas of the house. "I... I don't know what to do."

"Zac, man, get him off before he kills me."

Ian had only introduced the two of them for the first time a few days ago, but in that small amount of time, he'd come to like and even trust Lyle. After all, if not for the dog's nose, Bobby would have no doubt murdered his roommates.

Lyle's nose had led him to the trailer, to a home he had no reason to suspect. He'd smelled their scent on the ground and done what neither Tommy, Zac, or the other local shifters could do.

"They're right," Zac whispered despite the apple-sized lump in his throat. He tried to swallow it down, convincing himself what they were doing was for the best. "We'll tie him up and question him. You can let me go, Maiara. If you're innocent, Darrell, there's nothing to worry about, and this'll all be over in a couple minutes."

"You don't believe me? You're going to let this mutt tell you lies about me?"

Where had the fear gone? A moment ago, wide and terrified brown eyes had pleaded to Zac for aid. Now there was only simmering fury.

Something in Darrell's expression had changed, like removing a mask to reveal the true expression beneath. A cold gleam replaced the panic in his eyes. Before anyone could make a move toward him, a thunderclap boomed within the house.

The coonhound flew across the room and struck the wall with a yelp. Darrell leapt to his feet and thrust both hands out toward them. A wall of force slammed into Zac and knocked him backward. Maiara growled from behind him and leaned into the buffeting wind, strong enough even in her human form to resist the warlock's power.

Power flowed from Darrell's wristwatch. Lances of electric power raged between them, crackling in the open space and reaching out toward anything technological within reach. The television screen exploded, as did the computer nearby, each one creating a chain effect that branched into a dozen more streams of power.

"River," Zac called. He tugged at his shirt, torn between shifting and remaining human.

There wasn't enough room for Maiara and Zac to maneuver around the den to avoid the electrical field sizzling through the air, especially since it wasn't one of the rooms they'd recently expanded by knocking down walls. The acrid odor of burning carpet fibers filled the air, and spells left scorch marks against the rug beneath their feet. River jumped forward between Darrell and the shifters and swept both hands out, creating a magnificent shield glowing with opalescent light. Hues of ivory, pink, and pastel colors glimmered in the mystical aura.

An ebony cloud surrounded one of Darrell's fists. The malevolent, nebulous sphere pulsed then swam over them like a tidal wave of cold ink, blotting out Zac's vision of his surroundings and muffling the sounds in his ears.

No matter where Zac moved or where he stumbled, the bizarre darkness persisted.

"I can't see," Maiara cried.

"It's a sensory deprivation curse," River called back. She gritted her teeth, the grinding noise reaching Zac's ears despite the noise reduction effect of the curse.

The magical effect had even altered Zac's sense of smell, giving everything nearby a bland scent.

"I'm sorry, Zac." Darrell's voice resonated from every corner of the room, impossible to pin down. It was like listening to sounds underwater. "It wasn't personal, dude."

"You murdered people! Let Bobby get turned. You don't think that's personal?" He'd read the police report of what had happened to Pam Wiggins, and the knowledge of what Darrell had done sickened him. "What you did to that woman and her kid is as personal as it gets."

Lyle whimpered in the dark, the dog taking quiet, subdued breaths.

"You think I liked doing that? It was all about the power. I need it."

"You're a disgrace to all our kind," River snapped.

Darrell's bitter laughter created tension in Zac's spine. "I'm a disgrace? You know what's disgraceful? The way those high and mighty bitches treat the rest of us who don't fit into their agenda. That's a fucking disgrace. They don't care about you."

"You're wrong."

"Yeah? Then what have they done to help you with *me?*" Darrell challenged. His mocking laughter rumbled through the destroyed living room.

River had no answer for the dark witch, but Zac felt her beside him. Small sparks glittered around her wrist and created scant light, a pale green glow against her face. Her brows wrinkled with consternation.

"That's what I thought. Stay out of my way, River. I don't want to hurt you, but I will. Drop this whole investigation and none of you will have to die. This is the final warning."

Another deafening boom sent them all to their knees in pain. A fine network of cracks branched throughout River's shield, and then it dissipated entirely.

"He's gone." Zac growled, torn between going after his traitorous friend and staying to help. River's low, quiet groan made the decision for him. He moved to her side and helped her to her feet.

"Take it easy," he said when she swayed.

"I'll be okay. Just a little disoriented." Her favorite jade bangle lay in three distinct pieces on the floor at their feet.

Maiara hurried to Lyle and knelt beside him. The dog hadn't moved from the wall, but his tail feebly thumped against the ground.

"Oh no," River breathed. She rushed to join her and crouched beside their fallen friend. "Is he going to be okay?"

For a woman so large and muscled, Maiara could be surprisingly tender. She stroked Lyle's brow and glanced up at them. "I sense he is hurting very much, but he should recover from his injury. A broken bone or two is no big deal for a shifter."

Zac glanced up from their injured friend to the ceiling fixture in the foyer. With all the lights blown, they relied on moonlight filtering in through the windows. But even in the dark, he could tell River was crying, and for that, he could barely swallow the rage bubbling inside him. He wanted to track down Darrell and pull him apart limb by limb, not only for violating their friendship, but also for hurting River and disrespecting her home. "What do we do now, Riv?"

"We need to notify Dusty and Ian about what we're facing. We need to warn everyone about the danger."

"And then what?" Zac asked.

"I dunno... Dusty can make up a story that Darrell snapped and came in here with a gun or something. Attacked us with a weapon, hit our dog, I don't give a fuck what we have him say as long as no one else is hurt by that monster."

River stepped away from them, raking both hands through her thick curls before she disappeared around the corner leading to their circuit breaker box.

After he and Maiara got Lyle onto the couch and beneath a blanket in his human form, Zac hurried toward the utility room to find his girlfriend. River had leaned against the wall with her eyes closed.

"Riv? You okay?"

"I don't get it. I just don't understand how he had so much power and none of us noticed it. I *always* notice other witches, Zac. Always. I sensed things were up with Lucia even before I saw her dump a love potion in your wine."

"River, baby, don't blame yourself for this. None of us ever suspected him of being anything more than a normal human. Hell, he didn't do a damn thing at the Sin Den to fight against the vamps..." Zac trailed off as a startling realization dawned. "Fuck."

"What?"

"That's how they knew we were going to be there. Darrell must have told them."

"Then there's no telling what else he's shared with them."

**

River had never spoken so much on a phone in all her life. While Zac's Jaguar zipped down the road toward the Atropos Police Department, she made frantic phone calls to all the pals in his cell phone contacts.

"Call Patrick too," he growled after she ended a call with Ian. "Let him know this bastard can't be trusted."

"Okay." Her fingers trembled as she selected the address. She hated to be the one to share the devastating news, but Zac never chatted on the phone, and his fingers were so white-knuckled from his grip of the wheel she didn't want him to steer while distracted.

Darrell had been a good friend to him, a close friend their entire circle had trusted. She felt sick for them all, unable to comprehend the harsh blow dealt by the betrayal.

Over and over, she relayed the tale to the people closest to them before arriving at the station.

Dusty didn't question them or call the identity of the warlock into doubt. Before the hour ended, photographs of Darrell had been transmitted to every police station in central Texas, small and large.

"We'll connect him to the Wiggins murders too. That'll light a fire under everybody to have him found. Once the news runs with the story, everyday people will know to keep clear of him if they recognize him out in the open."

"What about evidence?" River asked.

"We'll lie," the man said grimly. "First time I've ever done it in my career, but I'll be damned if I let this murderer get away because he's magical. We'll plant what we need to. I have Judge McKinley signing a warrant right now to search this animal's apartment. Now, what are your witches going to do?"

"I don't know," River admitted. "But as soon as I do have details, trust that you'll be the first one to find out,

Dusty." Pythia hadn't answered the phone, so she'd been forced to leave a message.

The conversation with Dusty didn't last much longer, although it took her another hour to sketch out wards in the police station window frames with a Sharpie. Since lines of salt wouldn't be enough to keep Darrell out, she had brought a few personal magical defenses along and hung them on the door knobs. Attuning spell scroll ribbons to deflect Darrell wasn't hard when he'd left his stinking magical essence imprinted on her bangle during the fight.

Afterward, Zac drove them home while River made two more attempts to reach Pythia.

At the end of their residential street, they were the only house on the cul-de-sac, aside from the adjacent duplex Zac had purchased when their elderly neighbor moved in with his family across town. It lacked furnishings, and they primarily kept it empty to enjoy naked romps in their backyard. River's modest four-door sedan occupied the left driveway, but a sophisticated, cherry red Corvette with pitch black windows had been parked by the curb.

Maiara stood in the open doorway with her arms crossed over her chest. Two tall, slim figures dressed in all black faced her. River couldn't make out much more than that from the car.

"Our vampire guests?" Zac asked.

"Probably. We should get this over with."

They got out from the car and started up the walkway side by side. Zac radiated unease, and River was certain he'd shift in an instant if either of their guests so much as twitched in a way he didn't like.

"What's going on here?" Zac called as they approached, his loud voice booming across the small stretch of manicured lawn and summer flowers dividing them.

"They have insisted I allow them in," Maiara called over. "I insisted they will lose their arms if they try."

"Thanks, Maiara, I appreciate it. I'm River Jackson and this is my home. Who are you?"

Both figures turned as one in an eerie syncopation that raised the hairs on her nape. In the dim lighting, they looked like exact copies of one another, from their upturned noses to their chin-length red hair. It took her another moment to realize one was a man and the other a woman, because both were fine-boned and androgynous in identical suits. The breadth of the male's shoulders, and the woman's chest provided the only defining features.

"I am Sir Magnus Carmichael," the first one said.

"I am Dame Magnolia Carmichael. Lord Tremaine sent us."

"You're late," River snapped, in no mood to attempt a diplomatic approach. "You were supposed to be here yesterday."

The vampire twins looked at one another then back to her. They each wore a thin smile.

"An urgent matter forced us to remain indisposed. However, we are here now and prepared to serve," Magnolia said. "May we come in?"

"I'd feel better about talking to you both out here," River replied.

"Our home was attacked only hours ago," Zac added in a rare show of tact. "I hope you can understand our reluctance to allow anyone else inside."

"This is hardly an appropriate venue to discuss delicate matters," Magnus disagreed.

River mimicked Maiara's stance and crossed her arms over her chest. "Too bad. This is what we've got to work with. Now, have you found out anything about our friend or not?"

"The vampire? Yes. If we could see him, perhaps we—"

"He's not here."

Magnolia blinked at her. "Where is he?"

"Somewhere safe, and that's all you need to know."

"Our orders are to bring the neophyte to Rosenhaven," Magnus said.

"Well, we're going to have to deny you. We aren't at liberty to reveal his location since we don't know where he was taken." After the recent betrayal and observing Zac's pain, the smug bitch in River was itching to come out, even if the diplomatic part of her psyche screamed for her to be polite and respectful. "I don't see what removing him to Rosenhaven has to do with the rest of what's going on. It's clear he was targeted due to his connection to *me*."

"We have not determined much regarding who turned him," Magnolia told them. "Rosenhaven did not authorize—"

"Look, I'm getting tired of the same canned lines. You didn't authorize it, so go find out who broke the rules. That's why you're here, right? That's three vampire attacks in less than a week. The Sin Den, Club Delirium, and our friend."

"Yes," Magnus said. His fair brows pinched together. "Our investigation of the Sin Den delayed our arrival. As you know, we're unable to operate during daylight, limiting our time greatly during the summer months. Had we been able to arrive earlier without jeopardizing our own safety, we would have."

River relaxed her posture a smidgen. At least they had actually been doing their jobs. She cleared her throat and adopted a less aggressive tone. "Did your search turn up anything?"

The female vampire shrugged. "Nothing satisfactory. We questioned employees who had emerged from the thrall, of course, using our own unique gifts, but too much time has passed to determine anything of value. After all," she said, white teeth flashing, "you left no remains behind."

"However, based upon the descriptions given, we could guess the identity of one."

"It's a start," Zac said. "Who?"

"The brunette dancer you described," Magnolia replied. "She was a young adept who departed Rosenhaven on less than friendly terms last year. She was sent to Dallas to live with a more rigid coven. They reported her missing a month ago, but we had no reason to believe she had returned to the area."

Zac cracked his knuckles. "Right. So you didn't get anything else from the recovered thralls?"

"Nothing. Their minds had been tampered with, and anything they claim is inadmissible even by our law. It takes a vampire of tremendous skill with centuries of experience to unravel a mortal's brain after they've endured a compulsion."

"Shit," Zac muttered. "Okay, what about the vampire at the source of this? River has been trying to get information about Emma Whittaker for days now, with no luck."

Dead eyes. River didn't like them because the twins had dead eyes, but she hadn't met enough vampires in her short life of thirty-two years to know whether it was a common trait or not.

"I can confirm Emmaleigh Whittaker departed the state of Texas a year ago, and has yet to return. We're unable to divulge anything more about her whereabouts. Matters of privacy, you must understand," Magnus said, his matter-of-fact tone grating on her nerves.

"Can you tell us why she left?"

Magnolia's lips thinned. "Our kind find that, after a time, we wish a fresh start and a new life elsewhere. Our faces become too familiar when we remain in the same place."

"Emmaleigh had been a resident of the San Antonio area for six decades, however, and was long overdue for a change," Magnus added.

"Did she have anything on file regarding, I dunno, um, vampire children or thralls? Anything like that?" River asked, hoping to get any tidbit they'd throw her way.

"Emmaleigh has no approvals or requests on file for turning anyone. She also did not keep thralls, but she did have one registered feeder."

River's stomach churned a little.

"Explain what you mean by registered," Zac said.

"Each vampire of adept rank or above is allowed to register two mortals as their private chattel. One Joseph Wiggins has been recorded in the books as property of Emmaleigh and not to be harmed or used. So you see, Ms. Whittaker could hardly be your suspect in this awful murder. Direct family members are included by association."

Damn. Emmaleigh had been her strongest lead, her only one, in fact, until Lyle exposed Darrell's identity. Her shoulders deflated, but she forced her chin to remain high while staring down the two knights. "All right. You've cleared up a lot of things for me, so it's only fair to warn you that there's a warlock loose in town."

Magnolia smiled. "We have already been made aware."

"Yeah, but we know who it is," River said, renewing both vampires' interest in the matter. Ginger brows rose and cool eyes grew lively. "His name is Darrell Tyler."

"And you were going to share this information when?" the female vampire demanded, voice rising an octave, just short of shrill. Finally, some emotion.

"We only found out tonight," Zac said. "Hence the reluctance to let you into our trashed house."

Not that River thought he would have allowed the pair of vampires inside any other time. Revoking permission was a damned pain in the ass and not nearly as easy as Hollywood made it seem.

"We will send word if we discover anything else, but without access to the—to your friend," Magnolia said after a brief pause, "I do not think we will find the vampire responsible. You have my apologies, as well as our sympathy. Undergoing the change without consent is never easy."

"Please do what you can."

River and Zac stepped aside. They waited until the knights reached the curb before they headed inside, while Maiara lurked on the porch and stared the vampires down. She didn't budge, motionless and poised for trouble even after they shut the Corvette's doors.

"I don't care how much closer it would put them to identifying the person behind this. I don't want them anywhere near Bobby," Zac said once the creepy twins drove away. He peered through the window and frowned, thick brows drawn close together beneath his mop of dark hair. "Just saw a couple ravens take off after them, so I think Harrison's cousins are on the job."

"How long were they here waiting?" River asked.

"Ten minutes, no more," Maiara replied.

"They had a sweet ride at least," Lyle said, shattering the awkward tension. "Would have killed to get under that hood."

An involuntary smile snuck onto River's face. "How are you feeling now?"

"A little better. Sorry I wimped out on y'all like that."

Zac snorted and sat on the arm of the couch beside the injured man sprawled across the cushions. "Wimped out? Dude, you did everything you could until he took you out of the fight. He got the best of all of us. Now, you want help into the shower or do you wanna just lay there a while longer? Up to you, but River has this stuff you can pour into a bathtub that makes you feel like a thousand bucks."

"Thousand bucks would be nice. I feel like I was hit by a Mack truck and dragged a couple miles."

Zac helped Lyle, leaving River to survey the damage to the house. The whole living room was trashed, their fifty-five-inch television busted, with a network of deep fissures in the glass. Her boyfriend's expensive gaming PC—thankfully not the one where she did all her graphics design work for her clients—still smelled like burning parts. Nothing electronic in the room could be salvaged.

River tilted her head up to assess the ceiling and cringed. It would need painting to remove the black marks, but at least it hadn't cracked. There was always a silver lining, and things could have been worse. They could be boarding up shattered windows or out of a home altogether.

"I'll haul the rug outside," Maiara said.

"Thank you, Maia, but you don't have to do that. I'll clean it up after I make a few calls."

"I don't, but I want to," the bear said. Her warm smile put River at ease, and then she resumed tidying the ruined living room. Maiara had already swept up most of the glass and rolled the rug into a tight cylinder to be removed.

"I'm just glad my computer wasn't in here," she muttered. At Maiara's puzzled look, she added, "I work from home doing digital art. I back up often and all, but the recent stuff would have been lost."

The bear shifter gestured toward the desktop computer in the corner of the room. "Then whose was that?"

"Zac's, but he doesn't do anything on it aside from play PC games. He'll just use it as an excuse to buy another one that costs twice as much." Glancing at the smashed television brought a tiny smile to her face when she imagined Zac trying to sell her the idea of replacing it with the eighty-six-inch behemoth he'd seen online.

"All your things…"

"Replaceable," River said. "I'm only glad no one was seriously hurt." But seeing their home in shambles struck a blow to her morale, as did knowing their friend, a man they'd had over countless times for grill-outs and game day celebrations, was capable of such betrayal and so much senseless evil.

"True. Go make your phone call. I've got this." Maiara squatted beside a pile of trash and swept it into a dustpan.

"Okay. I'm going to report this to the council. One way or another, they're going to listen."

With the others occupied, River slipped into her private office and went over Pythia's head again, for the second time.

"River?" Rhona's voice had a heaviness in it, as if she'd roused from bed to take the call. As one of the elder witches on the Circle of Seven, their judgment council who held regional jurisdiction over the area, Rhona often dealt with witches who made infractions against their law.

"Sorry, I know it's late."

"Only a bit. What can I do for you, sweet?"

"We discovered who the warlock behind the murders is." Before Rhona could push her off on another witch, she spilled the entire story, from the discovery of the Blood

Sacrament to Darrell's exposure as the warlock they'd sought since October. At least, she was optimistic enough to hope he was the same one. If there were two in the area, they were screwed in ways she didn't know how to describe.

Rhona gasped. "I can't believe he's operated in Atropos for so long, but I suppose if he's become a master at cloaking his ability, it would make sense. Oh, this just makes me sick, love. Have you spoken with Pythia? She's been handling all matters in your town. It's her territory."

"I can't get ahold of her, so I'm calling you. I need to speak with one of the Trinity," River insisted. "I'm not taking no for an answer on this, Rhona. I want an audience and I want it now. I also want every witch from here to El Paso on the lookout for this bastard."

"Of course."

"And I… what?"

"I will make the arrangements, my dear. I wish you'd called earlier, because Pythia didn't mention a thing about any of this. My *word*, this is awful."

Her belly dropped to her knees, turbulent with nausea. "Nothing?"

"Not a word. I mean, of course, we all knew you were working on the Blood Sacrament investigation, but I assumed Pythia had the lead and you were assisting, since she asked us to limit our help to you."

"Limit your help?"

"Oh… Erm, I'm not supposed to say much about that. Anyhoo, dearest, I'd have checked in sooner if the Mother herself hadn't set all of us onto other tasks. You wouldn't believe the mess in El Paso right now."

Rhona continued to talk and blather, but it went in one ear and out the other. There was only one reason for Pythia to keep vital information to herself without informing the rest of the council, but the idea—the merest possibility— left her cold and trembling inside.

"Call me as soon as you get the meeting set up," River whispered, numbed. "Goodbye, Rhona."

***

Unable to sleep after the day's revelations and the drama of chasing a psychotic warlock across central Texas, River tossed and turned in bed. Zac had passed out, asleep beside her in his boxers, tucked beneath the blankets on his side of their shared bed.

Now that she knew the identity of the town's tormenter, she'd had to change all her wards and wasn't leaving anything up to chance. Before going to bed, she'd recreated and rearranged a dozen protective spells and charms. It would take an army to storm her house now, guaranteed to be warlock and vampire proof, as long as they came armed with anything less than a tank and some heavy ordnance. Despite that and three anxious shifters ready to do damage to the first threatening thing to step foot on her property, she still couldn't rest.

Surrendering to her insomnia, River slid from the bed and donned her robe. After checking each ward and protective spell in place around their home, she returned to bed beside her boyfriend and watched his chest rise and fall in the peaceful rhythm of sleep.

"Everything okay?" Zac asked without opening his eyes.

River jumped, startled. "Yeah."

"No, it isn't. What's wrong?"

"Nothing."

"The hell something isn't wrong. You've been tossing and turning for an hour."

"One of your best friends is a warlock and has been doing evil under my nose for years without me picking up on it. I'm a failure."

"No." Zac rolled to his side then sat up. "You're many things, River, but a failure isn't one of them."

"But, Darrell—"

"Fooled us all. Even Tommy never suspected, and he has a better nose than me. Darrell masked his magic well, managing to operate without any of his closest friends knowing something was going on, and made fools of us all. But even with all that, it's not our failure."

A shuddering breath quaked her shoulders and she dropped her chin to her chest. Zac slid his fingers into her hair and cupped her cheek in his warm palm.

"Hey," he said. "Don't do this to yourself. Don't take this burden."

"I know you're right," she whispered, looking up into his face. "But it's more than just Darrell's betrayal. We're supposed to be planning a trip. Enjoying our summer. Instead, we're battling vampires and chasing the worst sort my kind have to offer."

Even the soft press of his lips against her brow failed to soothe her worries.

"We'll still do those things," he promised. "They'll just be a little later than we planned. But that's not all that's bothering you."

Sometimes she thought Zac knew her better than she knew herself. How she had ever gotten so lucky was beyond her.

"You a mind reader now?" she asked.

"Nah, but I can recognize when you're distracted. C'mere."

He pulled her in close and guided her back down to the bed until they were lying side by side, face to face. His hand settled on her hip and his fingers traced little circles over her skin beneath her shirt.

"Tell me what's *really* bothering you."

"I guess I also miss talking to Pythia," she murmured. "Normally, I would have asked her for advice about all of this, but she has everyone shunning me out of the sisterhood and avoiding my calls. This must be how it feels to be excommunicated from the Catholic church or something."

Zac's brows pinched together. "Is she still out of town?"

"I have no idea. I'm assuming so, but without being able to talk to her, your guess is as good as mine."

"Did you tell her about your sudden level-up?"

"I told her about the sun spell, but she didn't say much. Just read me the riot act about getting involved with the vampires." After a pause, she added, "This isn't a videogame."

"True, but if it was, you'd be grinding experience to solo bosses right now."

"Ha. Ha."

"No, I'm serious. Don't you think it's a little strange that all your fellow witches are now unavailable, no matter what happens? Attacked by vampires in a garage, no one cares. You identify the evil fucker they wanted you to catch, no one cares."

River shifted against him, rolling Zacarias to his back beneath her so she could rest her arms against his chest. She studied his face. His green eyes glinted in the muted moonlight filtering between the shades. "What are you suggesting?"

"Something is very wrong in Atropos, and all of it isn't because of this warlock. I think your fellow witches have some questions to answer."

"Yeah, well, they're all keeping mum. I'm on my own. At least magic-wise."

"Then maybe we need to lean on them until we get information. I don't need to be a witch to know nothing about this is typical. Even Ian agrees, and we're ready to have your back if you need us."

She buried her face against his throat and kissed his beating pulse. "Thank you."

CHAPTER 12

True to her word, Rhona returned River's call in the early hours of the morning to inform her of an arranged meeting with the Mother. Her noontime appointment would be at the coven's preferred meeting place in San Antonio, so River hopped out of bed and hustled to get a few things done before she needed to leave.

"I don't like the idea of you going alone," Zac grumbled while he unloaded dishes from the washer.

"This is coven business. It's better that I go alone."

"Still doesn't mean I like it."

She lifted to her toes and gave his cheek a quick kiss. "I'll be back long before dark, I promise. And if this meeting doesn't go well... Well, I guess we'll cross that bridge when we come to it."

"Good luck."

"Thanks."

During the drive to the city, she practiced what she was going to say. Whoever the Mother was, River intended to demand answers and help. She refused to be patted on the head and set aside again in the dark.

The Witch's Brew Teahouse occupied a corner lot in a busy shopping plaza. River parallel parked on the street then headed inside the two-story building. A bell chimed as the door opened and closed, and then the fragrance surrounded her. Overwhelmed by the aromatic blend of every tea imaginable, she closed her eyes and stood breathing it in.

An ingenious use of magic ensconced her consciousness, the subtle spell woven into the air to relax visitors upon arrival. Her gaze swept over the sales floor, separated from the tea room by hand-painted sliding screens. A young witch smiled from behind the counter at River where she was assisting an elderly couple with a custom blend.

"Be with you in a moment, ma'am."

"Take your time. I'm here for the private room."

Upon receiving the code word, the girl's eyes lit with interest. She gestured toward a curtained doorway in the back.

River knew the way. Full coven meetings weren't held often, but she'd been to three in the past five years. She followed the hallway past the bathrooms to a locked door on the left. A repelling charm veered any wanderers away from the door, but she passed through it with ease and set her hand against the symbol etched into the frame. A rune flared to life beneath her palm, and then the door clicked open.

The stairway led up to a large, open room that encompassed the entire second floor. Bookshelves lined the walls to her left and right. Sunlight streamed in through three skylights overhead and beeswax candles burned on the altar at the opposite end of the space.

A woman with waist-length blonde hair stood with her back to River, silver strands twined throughout the golden plait.

Although she'd exchanged correspondence with the Mother and the Crone once before, she'd never met either of the three in person before. She wiped her sweaty palms against her leggings and stepped forward.

"Hello," River called uncertainly. She hung back a few steps and waited until the older witch turned to face her. The magical imprint of her aura had a haunting, familiar quality.

The other witch turned, bearing a fragile smile edged by laugh lines. "Good afternoon, River. Have a seat."

"Pythia?" She stared at her mentor, emotions conflicting. "I thought you were out of state. That you couldn't help me."

The older witch's smile faltered and faded away. "I returned late last night from Massachusetts."

The excuse seemed empty and hollow after everything that had been said on the phone. River's frown deepened and she tried to quell her rising nausea.

"I was supposed to be meeting with the Mother," River said.

"Yes, I know."

"Then why are you here? Did they send you because you're my mentor? Are you going to tell me yet again that you can't help?"

"No one sent me. Except myself, I suppose."

Rivers brows drew together. "I don't understand. Isn't she here yet? Is she even co—" She stopped, struck mute by a sudden realization, and stared at her long-time friend. "It's you, isn't it? You're Mother."

"Come have some tea with me. I brewed your favorite."

Tea. River stayed where she was as Pythia crossed over to a small table with cushioned chairs. A teapot with cherry blossoms painted onto the white glaze sat between two matching cups and saucers. It all seemed so normal, like any other time they'd sat down together for tea.

"How long?" River blurted without taking a single step.

"River, please," Pythia entreated. "Come sit with me and I will explain everything. You have my word."

The sadness in her friend's eyes drew her forward, though she remained stiff as she took her seat. Her unease was at odds with the familiar comfort she always found in Pythia's presence.

"I ascended from Maiden to Mother the year before you joined us," Pythia replied while filling their cups. She passed over the little cup of rock sugar. "I may not have given birth, but I feel as if all of you are my children. I love each of you equally."

She didn't trust her shaking hands with the delicate china, so River ignored her tea and kept her hands folded on the table. "Why me? I mean, I didn't think any of the Trinity actually mentored anyone."

"We don't. Not usually, at least. But you are a special case."

"Me?" Her voice squeaked upward in volume and pitch.

"Yes, but I think that bit of this conversation can wait until you report what you came here to say. Don't you?"

"Now you want to listen?"

"Oh, River…" Pythia reached across the table and set her hand over River's. "I know you're angry—you have every right to be—but right now we need to work on stopping this warlock and anyone he's working with. The message said you had discovered the man behind it all."

"We did, but I have a question for you first."

"Oh?"

River moved her hands out from beneath Pythia's touch and wiped her sweaty palms against her jeans. The question on the tip of her tongue made her sick to her stomach.

"Why doesn't the council know that I'm handling the case alone? Why is nobody helping me? Why…?"

"You believe I had something to do with it all," Pythia said, her voice quiet and heavy with sorrow.

"Can you blame me? I called for help and no one knew a thing."

"I hope you understand why now."

"Because you're the Mother?" River's laugh came out brittle and bitter. "What is this then? Some elaborate test you're torturing me with? No one should have to handle this alone, Pythia. No one. It's too damn big, and it's not fair of you to push it all off onto *my* shoulders. I deserve an explanation."

"Yes, you do, and I am here to give it to you." Pythia leaned back in her seat and folded her hands in her lap. "You're more than a witch, and more than a gifted sorceress. All this time we've led you to believe you're a prodigy, but the time has come to reveal the truth to you, River. We've held it long enough to protect you from those who would do you harm, but trouble seems to find you anyway. And given the recent development in your power, it would be unwise to maintain the secret any longer."

Her heartbeat kicked up a notch, a jackhammer thrum slamming inside her chest. "What do you mean? Pythia, you're scaring me. What the hell is going on? Why am I gaining all these powers overnight? I can cast spells without preparing them in advance or imbuing them in talismans. The other night I sensed a vampire who hadn't even completed his transformation."

"I know," Pythia murmured. "Rhona told me everything."

River's voice raised an octave, leaping to a shrill note as she continued. "A few days ago, I bottled *sunlight* without a recipe. I just… I somehow *knew* what to do. Ideas come to me now without ever cracking open my Book of Ways, like I have them all memorized."

The older woman held out both hands to quiet and calm her. "Shh… shh, love. I'm going to explain it all."

"Please do," River begged her.

"We've pushed you to develop your gifts at an unusual speed because we have no choice. There was no other way to escalate your awakening other than to place you beneath tremendous amounts of pressure—"

"My awakening?" River's voice cracked. "Just tell me what the hell is going on with me. Why was I able to create sunlight without a focus item like a magician when I have a witch's power to brew potions?"

With each conversation between them, Pythia grew more distant than ever. The formal aspect of their conversation sliced deep, inflicting a stinging wound to River's confidence. Had she done something to deserve losing her dearest, closest friend?

"We have reason to believe Hecate sent you to us."

"What?"

Pythia folded her hands together and spoke in a soft, reverent voice. "Several of our sisters have studied the stars for centuries awaiting a sign from the goddesses. And now, we think—no, we're certain you must be the second incarnation of Circe, come back to us after centuries of sleep."

A comet could have crashed down over them and she wouldn't have been any more stunned. Pythia was speaking gibberish. She had to be mistaken, or maybe she'd added something recreational to her tea and it was affecting her memory.

"But... no. No, that can't be right. I have no memories of another life. You all told me you were certain this was my first."

"We lied. I'm sorry, River. It was for the best until we could determine—"

"You lied to me? Lied to me about who I am then put me through the fucking wringer like an episode of *Naked and Afraid*? What kind of friend are you?"

"River—"

"No. I don't want to hear it." River jerked away from her mentor and stood. "You all threw me to the wolves, literally, now you want me to save your butts from whatever is happening here with powers I don't even understand."

"Sweetie, we never intended to throw you to the wolves. All of this was to test you and encourage personal growth. If for any reason, at any time, you had needed us, we were prepared to intervene."

"That's bullshit and you know it," she snapped. "I *called* for help. You told me not to get involved. When I was attacked by the vampires, you didn't give two shits. And now my home looks like a warzone because my boyfriend's *buddy* turned out to be the damned warlock terrorizing this town. You didn't help me then when I needed it. Were you even my friend at all, or was that another lie, because you needed to monitor me to see if I was your… your…" River couldn't even say it. Circe, the goddess Circe? They had to be wrong, but no matter how much she wanted to deny it, the sadistic theory made sense.

Moisture gleamed against Pythia's dark lashes. She blinked. "I have always been a friend to you, River. I only… I tried to do what was best. Had you truly been in need, I would have been there for you."

"I don't believe that. Not anymore."

"You're right about the issues in Atropos. If you could supply the proof we need to act against Rosenhaven, I'll have a dozen witches there before sunset. As the only other combat-trained witches in the immediate area right now,

I've asked Gloria and Rhona to search for this Darrell. I'll also personally join the hunt."

Iron determination straightened River's spine. Pushing her shoulders back, she met Pythia's gaze until her friend broke eye contact first. "I'd rather choke on glass than accept your help now, but that's not what's best for Atropos. Rhona will be my contact from now on, because I don't want anything else to do with you."

"River—"

"Nothing," she seethed. "Because what you've done to me is unforgivable."

Empowerment spread through River's veins as she stalked from the meeting chamber.

***

Unable to see the road clearly through her tears, River pulled over alongside the highway and wept until her chest heaved and her ragged breaths caused her to hyperventilate. All the time she'd loved and trusted Pythia, and it had all amounted to being nothing more than... than what?

What the hell was she to them? A goddess? Not merely a goddess, but one of the Goddesses with a capital fucking G, one of the preferred deities, beloved by all spell casters across the world who walked the path of good.

Her shoulders continued to shake, preceding a fresh wave of tears long after she thought she'd finally cried herself dry. She snatched handfuls of Kleenex from the box in her glove box and clumsily dried her face, thankful she hadn't worn makeup to make an even greater mess of herself.

Zacarias attempted to call her twice while she struggled to regain control of her emotions. She declined both calls with a generic auto-response text message that claimed she was driving.

Five minutes later, her phone rang again with her mother's name lit in the Caller ID. Desperate to speak to her mother, she accepted it.

"Finally!" her mother declared victoriously. "I've been trying for hours to return your calls. I thought I'd have to resort to the old ways and summon a wind spirit at this rate to carry a message for me."

"Mom," she sobbed into the phone, failing to control the tremors in her voice.

"River? River, baby, what's wrong? Why are you crying? What happened?"

"They said…" River dragged in a lung-filling breath. "They said I'm Circe. Said I'm one of the Goddesses, Mom. Is it true? Did you *know?*"

"I…" Her mom hesitated, then sighed. "They told me it was a possibility when you were born, but I didn't know for sure. Quite frankly, I didn't *care*. Honey, you were always my baby girl. That's the only thing that mattered to me."

Her mother's words inspired a fresh wave of tears. River swiped at her face and tilted her head back against the headrest. "But how did they know?"

"The usual oracle mumbo-jumbo. Star alignments, celestial activity on the night you were born. But I didn't care. You were the first baby I've ever had in all of my lifetimes, and nothing they said mattered to me."

"Thanks, Mom."

"What's going on, baby?"

She started from the beginning, leaving nothing out, and ended with her discovery of Pythia as the Mother. Maybe she wasn't supposed to reveal that last bit, but she didn't care anymore about their petty secrets.

"I'll try to gather the ingredients to make a teleportation circle. Chris won't mind if I—"

"No, no. You're on a cruise." She sniffled. "And I don't think you'll find malachite powder and ground fulgurite on a ship in the middle of the ocean."

Cynthia sighed. "You're right. But I hate the idea of you handling all this alone."

"I'm not totally alone. I have the local shifters with me, and Rhona will do what she can, I'm sure."

"The mark of a great leader is reflected in who is willing to follow you, River. If the shifters are there to help you, I feel better about you undertaking this task for the Circle. No matter who Pythia believes you to be."

"I love you, Mommy."

"I love you too, baby. I'll be there at your side as soon as this ship reaches port."

CHAPTER 13

The smell of fresh paint filled the house. River picked her way through the hall, squeezing past the furniture that had been pulled out, and stepped into the living room. Drop cloths dotted with cream paint covered the floor, and Zac had a roller on a pole. Each swipe he made across the ceiling covered the scorch marks, but he hadn't yet concealed the black streaks across the mint green walls.

"Looking good," she called out. "I like the color."

Zac grinned down at her from the short stepladder. "Figured we might as well get that new paintjob done now, since you weren't feeling the white anymore."

"Is this *all* you've done the entire day?" she teased.

He rolled his eyes. "Well, Tommy and I ran out to check all of Darrell's usual hangouts, but we didn't see any sign of him."

"If he's smart, he's left town. He knows what I am and that I would have called the council in."

"He won't leave town, because whatever he's doing is centered on Atropos. Well, I mean, he can't leave town *permanently*. He's gonna be back. We all know that much, but what I really wanted was to find any hint or clue alluding to what the hell he's planning to do. What's his endgame? Why does he need so much power?"

"True." A ragged sigh tossed her long bangs out of her face. What would she do without Zac's brainpower? "Where are Lyle and Maiara?"

"He was feeling better, so she went out with him on a walk to try to pick up Darrell's scent again. Harrison's providing aerial support along with a flock of his cousins, and Ian is on the road again. Should be arriving any minute."

"Oh, great." Ian's sensible outlook toward matters had been a blessing.

"So, now that you've been apprised of my activities, how did your meeting go?"

River didn't have to lie to Zacarias, but she didn't reveal the entire course of the conversation with Pythia either. Excluding the mention of her being a goddess seemed like a good idea, considering the simmering tension between them about the heap of work her sisterhood had piled on her shoulders.

And she couldn't blame him, really, for being upset about it all. She felt like their servant girl, taking on enormous duties of increasing importance with minimal support from the others. Then again, most witches weren't combat trained either. The average witch of the local covens knew how to brew potions, read palms, and create protective wards, but they didn't learn magical warfare.

If she really was Circe, what did that mean for her workload? What would be expected of her and how could she live up to their expectations?

Instead of telling him that he was dating a deity, she ranted about Pythia holding back on providing aid and her failure to provide full disclosure to the other witches in the area.

"So that's it. We're on our own," Zac said. He ran his hands through his hair before hugging her closer.

"Not exactly. Though we'd probably still be on our own if I didn't snap and give Pythia a piece of my mind." Had she overreacted?

She must have worn her regret in her expression, because Zacarias frowned. "No, you were right to tell her off," he said. "If the witches really wanted to help, they should have jumped into this from the beginning instead of sitting on their magical hands while you carried the work."

"I know."

"Speaking of carrying the work... I have an idea," he began, "but I don't know if you're gonna like it."

"I'm willing to hear any suggestions right now."

"This is bigger than anything I've ever seen, and the town is at the eye of the storm. With Rosenhaven in our backyard, I think it's time we brought in more help."

River blinked up at him. "From where? We already have two wolf packs, and Maiara said the bears would help."

"I was thinking more local."

She scrunched her brow and pursed her lips while raking her mind over the groups of supernatural creatures she trusted. She hadn't yet made up her mind about the twin vampire knights. "Who else is there?"

"The Atropos Police Department. While we've been calling all these shifters and requesting help from the witches, we have an untapped resource sitting right here with the right to know about what's happening in their backyard. It's about time we let them know what's out there. Then we can show them how to combat it."

The idea was as crazy as it was brilliant. "Arm them with knowledge."

"Exactly. There's always one cop on duty at night in Atropos, and if he's in the dark about vampires, what's going to happen to him?"

"Death."

Zac nodded. "How much of that sunlight stuff did you brew? Is it ready yet?"

"I think so. I made five gallons of it, but I can brew more."

"Then I think we should stock the police armory with everything you can give them. Weaponize it in whatever vessels we can. Does it have to be in a glass vial?"

"No. Why do you ask?"

A big grin spread across her boyfriend's handsome face, crinkling the corners of his emerald eyes. "Good. I kinda hoped you'd say that." He crossed over to the closet at the foot of the stairs and opened it to remove a Super Soaker from the shelf.

River stared at him.

"Am I a genius?" he asked.

"The best kind of sexy genius."

With Zacarias's encouragement, she got on the phone with Dusty and shared their ideas with him. To her surprise, the chief didn't shoot down her idea. Ian arrived shortly after she returned to her brewing room to double their sunlight potion stock, so the two men drove off to clean out the nearest Walmart of every water gun they carried.

"Going to need more potion than this," River muttered, incapable of supplying the immense demand they'd need. If they wanted to arm the police department and all their shifter friends against an entire coven, they'd have to be prepared.

While the fresh batch simmered, she hurried to her home office and slipped behind the computer to type up her recipe. She selected Rhona's contact information from the address book and sent it before dialing the other witch.

"Hello, River," Rhona greeted her.

"Hi, Rhona. I need a favor."

"Name it, and I'll do my best."

"I know everyone isn't trained to fight, so I don't need combatants. I need the best alchemists we have to each prepare at least five gallons of the potion I just e-mailed to you."

"Hold on a moment, let me pull it up."

River waited, listening to the sound of keyboard keys clacking over the line.

"This is a sunshine tonic, except it's different than what I recall," Rhona said, puzzled.

"I improved the recipe. It now acts like a direct ray of sunlight. I need you to forward it on and get people started on it right away."

"Of course. I'll send this out and get my own batch started. Georgina can have twice that much to you within the week."

"No. Not a week. We need it tomorrow."

"Tomorrow?"

"I know it's short notice and it's a lot of work, but this is necessary."

"How many vampires do you think are involved?"

"I don't know, but I have a bad feeling about it. Better to be armed and overprepared than caught with our pants down again. My gut says there's a disagreement brewing at Rosenhaven, a split in factions maybe."

"And why do you think that?"

"The ex-husband of the victim Darrell sacrificed. He was a registered feeder for one of those vampires, but she blew out of town last year and left without warning. Also, I need you to do one more thing for me."

"Of course, my dear. Anything to help."

"I need to know the name of the witch tasked with discovering new talent. Contact all the circles across Texas and find out if anyone has trained or worked with him before. I want to know if he's made friends who may have similar dark beliefs. Maybe one of them is sheltering him."

"I'll get right on it."

"Thank you, Rhona."

With one part of her plan underway, River ended the call and prepared her speech for the Atropos chief of police. Hopefully Dusty saw the wisdom in their crazy plan.

***

"You're sure about this?" Dusty asked later that afternoon as River and Zac stood in front of him in his office.

She cringed when the chief spit a mouthful of tobacco into an old plastic cup on his desk. Zac's nose wrinkled. It probably smelled ten times worse to him. "Positive. But can you like... not do that? A little distracting, Dusty."

"Sorry, River. Habit. Anyway, I was under the impression your folk didn't much like for a lot of normal people to know you exist. What's changed now?"

As she thought about the lives lost so far, River pressed her lips together and struggled to compose her thoughts. The answer came more easily than she'd anticipated. "More lives are in danger now than ever before. There are bad vampires on the loose, a warlock carrying a supercharged magical battery, and no guarantee innocent people won't be harmed. I'll probably get in trouble for it, but I'll cross that bridge when I reach it."

"We have to do what's best for Atropos," Zac said. "The other shifters agree."

"All right. I called everybody in after you and I spoke on the phone. A couple of the guys are pissed about me ordering them here on a day off, but this is serious business."

"Where is everyone?"

"Conference room next door in City Hall. Only one big enough to hold everyone and do, uh, what you wanna do. I hope you know what you're doing, River."

"Me too," she mumbled as he led her and Zac next door.

The conference room wasn't much bigger than a typical classroom, with a single table running down the center and a dozen chairs with split upholstery revealing the battered cushioning. Four of the guys had taken seats, the other two in uniform and approaching the table.

"The hell is going on, Dusty?" Officer Roberts asked before he slouched back in a seat too small for his enormous girth. His shirt stretched over his round stomach and massive chest, and the fluorescent lights gleamed over the dome of his bald scalp.

"River wants to have a word with all of us about something important. Y'all know how things have been weird lately in town, right?"

"This have anything to do with why River was walking around our crime scene at the rec center?" Officer Duncan asked. Of the six-man police department, he was the scrawniest of them, a middle-aged man with a receding hairline beneath his blue baseball cap.

"It does," Dusty confirmed. "That's the start of this weirdness, right?"

One of the cops snorted. "Shit was weird in Atropos long before that," Officer Clark muttered before scratching his enormous stomach. "What's happening?"

"First, I'm going to ask both of you to set your firearms aside," Dusty said to the two on-duty police officers carrying their handguns. River shot him a fragile smile of appreciation. Good thinking. The last thing they needed was for one of them to freak, shoot first, and ask questions later.

"Zac, will you do the honors?"

Forewarned about her plans, Zac had worn a T-shirt and sweats. He pulled the shirt over his head and tossed it over the back of a chair.

"Uh," Duncan said before he scratched his balding head. "I'm not quite sure what kind of thing y'all called us here to do, but we need answers."

"And you're going to get them," River assured the man. "We're going to show you a lot of things that you probably won't want to believe. Magic."

"Magic?" Duncan asked. He snorted with laughter, joined by the other disbelieving officers standing alongside him. "Come on, what did you really ask us here for?"

"That's it," the chief said. "They're going to perform magic for you, and then I guarantee your lives won't ever be the same, gentlemen."

A couple of the guys glanced away when Zac dropped his sweatpants, but then he shifted, becoming the beautiful, all black panther she'd loved and appreciated since the first day she saw him traipsing through the forest behind their home. Well, loved after she was no longer at risk of peeing on herself out of fear because she thought a wild animal was on the loose.

"What the fuck?" Everyone jumped back in varying degrees, but one of the older cops hit the wall. A second bumped against the corner of the table. No one instinctively reached for their sidearms, at least, alleviating the tension in her chest.

"It's all right," River said. She stepped over and stroked Zac's head. "He's a shapeshifter, and he's not the only one living in Atropos."

"You mean to say we've got cat people in town? Like Stephen King's *Sleepwalkers*?" Officer Morales asked.

Zac chuffed, startling the young officer who asked the question.

River cracked a small smile. "He doesn't suck the souls out of virgins, so no, not exactly."

The same cop glanced at Dusty. "Chief, this is some sort of joke, right? Is someone pulling a Criss Angel and doing a magic trick? An illusion?"

Dusty hitched his thumbs in his belt loops. "I'm afraid not. Now, I wanted to protect you boys from the dark truth, but the fact of the matter is, I'm only putting you in more danger by not telling you what's out there. You are all now entrusted with the greatest secret in all of Atropos."

Officer Clark cocked a brow. "What happens if we don't keep this to ourselves?"

"You get witches, shifters, and things scarier than us on your trail wanting to silence you. It isn't worth it, believe me," River said in a gentle voice. "But we're telling you this because we trust you and want to keep this town safe. We can't do it alone anymore without putting innocent people at risk."

The absolute silence in the room over the next few minutes was deafening. River waited it out and tried not to let her apprehension show. Beside her, Zac bumped his head against her knee and then pushed his nose into her hand. After what seemed like an eternity, the men staring at them all gave solemn nods.

"What do we need to know?" Morales asked.

River released her pent-up breath. "A lot, actually. More than I can tell you in one sitting. But tonight, we're going to focus on vampires."

Officer Clark crossed himself. "For real?"

"Yeah. Now, first thing you need to know—and this is super important—is that not all vampires are a threat. Most of them are like you and me and just living day to day, er, or night to night. But like with any group, there are bad apples. And unfortunately, Atropos has come under attack from a bad group."

No one had freaked out yet. She studied their grim faces and waited until one of the men spoke.

"What the hell can we do against them then?" Morales asked. "Is it like the movies and shit?"

"Kinda. Sunlight is bad. Garlic is crap," she said before launching into the same primer she'd given Dusty at the rec center. By the end, their faces had begun to gleam with sweat, and a couple white-knuckled hands gripped the armrests of their chairs. "Bullets won't do a thing to older vampires. As they age, their bones become stronger and bullets won't penetrate their skulls. Also, crucifixes and holy verse are nonsense to them."

"Holy shit," someone whispered.

Zac chuffed before he moved away, disappearing into the restroom with his clothes in his mouth. Officer Duncan stared until the jag was out of sight, while River bit back a grin and focused on the issue at hand.

"Then what *can* we do against them?" Morales asked, among the first to recover from the shock.

"There are folk out there in the world who train for years to take out vampires. The problem is, they kinda hate witches and everybody else too, which means calling them here isn't a good idea," River said. "So, I've made these." She removed a handful of golden vials from the basket and sat the glowing bottles on the table. "Think of these as sunlight grenades. Where one shatters, it'll create a bright flash with approximately a twenty-yard radius and fill the immediate area with sustained sunlight for about ten seconds."

"Seriously?" Roberts leaned forward and picked up a single vial. "Will they kill them?"

"Vampires can't tolerate sunlight, especially young ones. One flash will be enough to turn them to ash. Older, stronger vampires might survive, but they'll run like hell. I've brewed a full cauldron of these and I'm leaving the basket here."

"What about stakes?"

River shook her head at Roberts. "It's not so easy to drive a stake through someone's chest. You'd be pummeled before you ever managed to break the skin. That means your best bet are these vials."

"Or one of these." Zac returned, a deluxe Super Soaker in his hands. "Fill one of these bad boys up and you have a gun that shoots sunlight. The bloodsuckers won't even get close."

"I'll be damned. You made liquid sunshine," Officer Clark breathed. "I always knew there was something funny about y'all in that house way down at the end of the lane. Buying up the property near you whenever it opens."

River shuffled in place and dropped her gaze to the floor, her face feeling hotter than it probably looked. Claiming the other houses had been Zacarias's idea most of all, but she hadn't regretted his decision to purchase the adjacent lots. She liked the privacy as much as he did. "Anyway, we're always available to answer questions."

The ball was in their court now, and all River could do was hope they took her invitation to heart. For a human without immense amounts of firepower or supernatural abilities, there was no greater advantage than knowledge. Or a couple rocket launchers, and something told her the cash-strapped Atropos Police Department didn't have access to those.

Chapter 14

River returned home to find Lyle and Maiara babysitting the twin knights. The former had an ash stake in his right hand and was idly flipping it end over end and catching it again. He had a Glock tucked into the waistband of his jeans, while Maiara stood with her arms crossed. Neither hid over the threshold and had greeted the vampires on the porch.

Awkward.

The moment Zac parked the Jag in the driveway, she sprang out of the passenger seat and sprinted over to meet them.

"Hey, y'all," Lyle greeted. "We were just telling these friendly knights about how we found vamps hiding in an old shack on the edge of town. Two of 'em in fact. Not too strong or big though."

A pulse of excitement zipped through River. Finally, a lead. "Oh?"

"Yeah. Too bad they came up fighting and startled us. One of 'em bumped into Maiara and had a little accident with the sun. Then the other kinda walked into my stake. Don't know how that shit happened. I kinda blame my left arm. Has a mind of its own sometimes, you know?" He flexed the black metal hand and glanced up to shoot the two tense knights a smile. Their placid expressions never faded.

"What led you to those vampires anyway?" Zac asked.

Lyle's teeth flashed when he grinned, appearing a little more canid than human as the porch light reflected over his face. "Caught a whiff of ol' boy Darrell's scent and convinced Maiara to join me in a little B&E. House wasn't inhabited by nothin' but those two, and they're just ashes now, so…" He shrugged.

"It would behoove our investigation, as well, if you'd find a way to restrain any vampires in the future," Magnolia said pleasantly. "We would like to identify them and determine their motives."

River fixed her attention on the knights. "I'm hoping that same investigation is why you guys are back here again. Do you have any news?"

"Yes. We followed up at Club Delirium and the drone at the counter has been questioned and detained. We believe him to be connected to your assault."

River's brows rose. "I'm pretty sure you've got the wrong guy."

Magnolia's eyes flashed. "And you believe this because…?"

"Because he was in my sight the entire time I was in that bar and there's no way he called down that many vampires to ambush me in the two minutes it took to walk from the bar to the car. Someone else is behind the attack."

"That is not what we discovered," Magnus replied. "The responsible party has been brought to Rosenhaven for punishment and we consider the matter closed."

"Excuse me?" Her voice rose sharply. "That's it?"

"Concerning the attack at Club Delirium, yes. We are still looking into the other matters. We will report when we have something of substance."

Their superior attitudes and blatant disregard for anything she said made River see red. Zac curled an arm around her waist as the twins sauntered down the drive and past them to their car. His grounding touch was the only thing keeping her from following and giving them a piece of her mind.

Lyle maintained his bright smile until the sporty Corvette zipped down the road. As soon as the vamps were gone and out of sight, he said under his breath, "Maybe it's the ex-con in me, but I don't like or trust them as far as I can throw either of them."

"Is it the ginger hair?" Zac asked, smiling weakly.

"You know it, kittycat." Lyle's brief grin faded as deep lines creased his brow. "All jokes aside, I didn't feel comfortable sharing the rest of our discovery while they were around. This guy, Darrell, his scent just picks up and stops at random all around town."

"Could be from driving places. I mean, we had his vehicle impounded, but that doesn't mean he couldn't have gotten another," Zac pointed out.

"No, I don't think that's it. Hear me out for a second, okay? Ian told me all about that shit last year with your ex-wife. She turned into a bat. I think this guy is doing something similar."

River touched the tiger's eye pendant hanging around her neck and considered the theory. "It's possible, I suppose, but what makes you think so?"

"I have a pretty good head for smells—I never forget one once it crosses my nose, but almost every time I encountered his scent out in town recently, there was this… odor like…" He wrinkled his nose. "Buzzard."

"Buzzard?"

Lyle nodded. "Buzzard. It explains how the hell he got away from us without leaving a trace last night. This morning, I felt like I could go on the trail, so I convinced Maiara to come out with me as backup. I mean, I'm tough and all, but I got triplets and a wife back home waiting for me, ya know?"

"How are the ribs, by the way?" River asked.

The dog shifter raised his shirt, revealing a mottled blue and green patch of discoloration on his right side large enough for River to cover with both of her palms. She winced. "I've had worse," he assured her without losing his grin. "This'll all be gone in a couple days."

"Still, I'd feel better if you take it easy."

The group stepped inside to escape the hot and muggy night. With the merciless Texas summer upon them, August weather had brought a host of mosquitoes and other evening pests. Once she'd had a moment of the cool, air conditioned current against her perspiring brow, River locked the doors behind them and checked the wards dangling from the door knobs. They looked like silk ribbons, but she'd written every spell painted on them.

"Who's ready for dinner?" Zac asked.

"God, yes," Lyle said, while Maiara laughed. "Any of last night's supper left for us?"

"Plenty of it," Zac assured him.

River's stomach rumbled, and all she could think about were the fajita leftovers awaiting her in the fridge since Zac had gone overboard and cooked enough for a dozen people the previous night.

Lyle yawned and meandered past her into the living room. The couch had survived the disaster, the cocoa brown microfiber requiring only a gentle wash with a damp cloth and bucket of suds. After setting his handgun on the coffee table, the dog shifter lounged back on the sofa. Zac had brought their bedroom television set down in the meantime, providing a way for their house guests to unwind.

"Are you supposed to have that?" River asked curiously, nodding her head to the Glock. She slipped into Zac's armchair and listened to him singing in the kitchen while he no doubt heated up the tortillas and made fresh sides.

"Have what?" She popped one brow up and stared until Lyle bashfully grinned. "Legally? No, but I can promise you Ian knows I have it. He gave it to me, actually, just when we were on our way out here to help y'all."

"Ian's a good guy," River said carefully.

"He is."

"So…" She rocked on her toes briefly, regretting her initial observation and question. Lyle had only helped them, risking his own safety in the process.

"You're wondering why an ex-con is helping you, right? It's cool, girl. I get it. I wasn't always like this, I guess. Back when Ian first met me, I was a real shithead. Doing and dealing drugs, causing trouble in my hometown. Damn near drove my own mother into an early grave. Then Ian and his friends sent me to prison. They saved my life," he said, tone surprisingly reverent.

"He got you out of that lifestyle."

"Yeah. And I was a bitter asshole when I got out. Ain't nobody had a reason to give a fuck about me, but that old man did. I guess you could say he saved me twice. Because of him, I got this," Lyle said, waving his left arm. The prosthetic didn't resemble anything she'd ever seen compared to modern technology in the field. "He led me to my wife, and now I have a family. I owe everything to him, so when he asked if I'd come along and help out, there wasn't any answer to give but a 'hell yeah' before I rushed off to pack my bags."

Maiara had settled on the other sofa, the bear shifter a silent observer of their exchange.

"How old are your kids?" River asked curiously.

"Just turned a year old two weeks ago."

"That must be a handful. Is your wife a shifter too?"

"Yeah. Coyote. She's actually the one who designed this arm. I know it's a bit of a drive, but if your guy ever needs to see a doc who knows what they're dealing with, my wife has her own clinic up in Quickdraw. Well, medical research facility. But she has everything a hurt shifter could need when it comes to getting fixed up."

"I'll remember that. Thanks."

"Anyway, I'm gonna go get a beer. Can I get either of you ladies something?"

River started to rise from her seat. "I'll get it for you."

Lyle waved her off. "He broke my ribs, not my legs," he told her with another big grin on his face. He passed under the arch and into the open entrance room, though he paused before passing before the foot of the stairs.

"He has an interesting story," Maiara said.

"He does. But we haven't heard anything about yours. Um, so... I've kind of wanted to ask for a while. Is English not your first language?"

A deep furrow lined Maiara's brow. "What makes you ask?"

"Your English is great. It's just, sometimes it's a little stilted."

A fleeting smile appeared on the bear's face. "English is my first language, but I did not learn it until five years ago."

"Huh? But you look like you're hardly out of your twenties. You didn't learn to speak until your teens?"

"It is a strange story."

"You don't have to share if you don't want to," River said in a rush. "I don't mean to pry."

"You are not. I am happy to share. It's only..." She spread her hands and gave a short laugh. "I am a bear first and a person second."

There were stories—old stories—that spoke of animals who took human shape. River had only met a handful of them, all of them wolves and members of Tommy's pack, since he and Argus had a fondness for them and had vowed to protect them. The younger alpha had even affectionately dubbed them wulfweres, reversing the term for their benefit.

Until now, River hadn't realized they came in other animal varieties.

"How old were you when you first became a human?"

Maiara spread her hands again. "I could not say for certain. They believe I was five or six years old. As bears, we have no need or desire to tell the time," she explained. "But I know I am happy now. And I am happy to have come and helped you for our leader. He said meeting more humans would be good for me."

"Well, I've certainly appreciated your help. Your friendship too."

"As have I."

Lyle's approaching footsteps approached and stilled near the stairs again. He sniffed the air then peered into the living room, crinkling his nose.

"What is it?" River asked.

"I smelled something funny. I swear it's every time I pass by here."

"Funny in what way?" River rose from the couch.

"I have not smelled anything unusual," Maiara said. She moved over to Lyle and sniffed. "A faint burn, like magic, but it is the same scent all over."

"See, I thought so too at first, but something about this area is slightly different. Subtle."

While River watched, Lyle turned around in a circle, his nose in the air and eyes closed. She could easily envision him in hound form spinning around and chasing his own tail, a thought that brought a smile to her face.

"I have lots of magical talismans around the house. Want me to look and see if anything is out of place?

"Not needed. I think I found the source of it." Lyle swept a pair of abandoned ear buds off the low table, the slim bundle of white cords tucked between. After a sniff and a grimace, he presented them to River. "It's these. They smell like—"

"Those are Darrell's earbuds." River snatched them up and turned them over in her hands. The magic around them was almost too subdued to be noticeable. She must have walked past them a dozen times or more, but now that she had them in her hands, the enchantment was unmistakable. He'd been eavesdropping through them.

"You sneaky little fucker," she muttered, then raised her voice into the mic piece. "I am going to get you for this, Darrell. You hear me? You messed with the wrong witch."

Smoke curled up from her fingertips and the delicate device went up in flames. Plastic and thin wires melted until the whole thing became a messy lump.

"Now we know how he was always ahead of us," Lyle said. "I'll toss this in the trash outside." He took the ruined earbuds and headed for the door.

River's morale reached a new level of rock bottom. Despite all their careful planning, her wards, and hours of spellcasting, their best course of action was to assume Darrell knew everything.

And any hopes they had of getting ahead of him had died.

***

Less than thirty minutes after Zacarias reluctantly left for the office, Harrison phoned River's cell. The agreement between the two shifters was for Harrison to perform surveillance above Atropos that morning, allowing the two men to exchange places. They'd both been up to their elbows in the dark business affecting the town and had fallen behind in their work.

They might have been the bosses, but they still had to direct their programmers if they wanted to keep their indie game development company up and running. Last she'd heard, they had a round of glitches to hammer out before their current project could leave the beta testing stage.

"What's up, Harrison?" River asked, tucking the phone between her ear and shoulder while she finished unloading the dishwasher.

"Hey, River. I think something's happening over here that you need to see, like now," Harrison rambled into the phone. It took her mind a few moments to interpret his rushed words.

"Over where? What's happening?"

"I was doing an aerial above town to look for anything out of place, like Zac asked me to do, but then I saw this like energy explosion rock through this subdivision on the outskirts of town. I'm pretty sure it came from Pythia's house. It's a wreck, dude. I returned to my clothes as fast as I could and called you."

"I'm heading over right now."

Plates clattered together as she set them hastily in the cupboard.

"Lyle, hold down the fort. I'm going to Pythia's."

"What's wrong?"

"An attack, from the sounds of it." She couldn't imagine her mentor causing the disturbance through a weird accident. Pythia was too skilled.

"I'll come with you."

"No, I need someone here."

"Then I will come," Maiara said.

River nodded without argument and snatched her car keys off the hook. Worry set off flutters and trembles through her entire body, and she dropped the keys twice before she managed to get the key in the ignition.

Now that they had the local police involved, she didn't worry about staying under the speed limit. She blew through the single stop sign on her street.

Please be okay, please be okay, she repeated in a silent prayer.

Although it took less than five minutes to cross town and reach the outskirts of Atropos, River felt the magical aura long before they arrived at the scene. Energy tingled against her skin a block before she screeched to a stop in Pythia's driveway. Curls of smoke still rose from the smoldering flowerbeds.

River clutched the car door to keep on her feet. "No…" She blinked, trying to hold back the tears. The entire area festered with dark magic and negative energy, wafting off the ruined framework of what had once been a beautiful ranch-style home.

She bolted away from the car and took off toward the backyard with Maiara on her heels. Everything had been burned. The trellis gazebo was a smoking husk.

"Pythia!"

"In there," Maiara called over. She stood beside the open French doors and gestured inside. River rushed over.

The interior of the house reeked of magic and had suffered the same damage as the gardens. Scorch marks covered the walls, and several pieces of furniture had been blown apart. The ceiling had collapsed, and a yawning hole in the rooftop revealing the overcast sky above. Beneath that wreckage, a pale white hand lay outstretched over the rubble-strewn carpeting.

"No, no, no…"

Working together, the women managed to clear the debris, although Maiara practically lifted the enormous pieces like they were made of Styrofoam. At the bottom of the mess, they found River's former mentor. Blood matted Pythia's hair at her scalp and scrapes covered her arms. While the shallow rise and fall of her chest meant there was still life in her, it didn't guarantee it would remain that way for long.

"Pythia?" River cried, hoping to rouse the older woman. When that failed, she fumbled her cell phone from her back pocket and dialed 911. "I need an ambulance. Please, my friend has been seriously hurt."

The wait for emergency services was agonizing, and River worried every moment that Pythia's breathing would stop. Each time the older woman groaned or gasped, River's heart skipped a beat.

"Hang in there, Pythia," she whispered. "Don't you dare die on me. Not like this."

"River?" Dusty's voice carried through from the front of the house.

"We are in the back," Maiara called.

River moved on autopilot, unable to answer his questions and barely aware of what was happening until the moment the EMTs loaded Pythia into the ambulance and tore down the road, sirens screaming.

"She will be all right," Maiara said in a low voice as she set her hand on River's shoulder.

"I hope so," she whispered.

Dusty returned to the patio and mopped his brow. "This is becoming a real mess, River. An attack like this isn't so easy to sweep under the rug and explain away."

Maiara glanced at the chief. "Arson. Say it was arson. You already have a suspect."

"That's the story I plan on. Look, River, I'm sorry about your friend. We're doing everything we can to locate Darrell, but he's like a goddamn ghost."

The reality hadn't quite sunk in, her mind unusually numb despite watching an ambulance take away the woman who had been, for all intents and purposes, a second mother to her since early adolescence. "I know,

Dusty," she spoke at last, unable to do more than offer a fragile, halfhearted smile of appreciation to Maiara. "And even if you do locate him, I don't want you guys to confront him. He'd kill all of you and wouldn't think twice about it."

He nodded. "Go ahead and do whatever you need to inside. I'm, uh, figuring my search methods won't turn up much, but I gotta at least make it look legit."

River dropped her shoulders. Going inside once was enough, and she'd gleaned everything she needed to know in those few minutes. "I already know why he came here and what this was about. My friend was keeping watch over a prisoner. A dangerous witch prisoner, and her cage isn't in the rubble anywhere."

Now she understood why Pythia had taken the dark witch into her care to serve out her punishment in the form of a bat.

"Shit," Dusty muttered. "This gets worse by the second. Does this have anything to do with that mess from last year when my men were called out to your residence?"

"It does. I think our warlock came here to free her, and if he's gone through the trouble to rescue her, he knows how to undo her self-transmutation spell."

Maiara's mouth flattened into a grim line. "Which means our work has become more complicated. We no longer have one dark witch to find, and must now locate two."

"Exactly."

CHAPTER 15

L ucia had known all along that the master wouldn't abandon her, but in those recent months of imprisonment, there had been moments of doubt when she wondered if she'd served her purpose to him and had no further use. Had he forgotten her?

Occasionally, she'd heard snatches of conversation among the witches who contacted the blonde bitch holding her captive, but her warden prevented her from hearing anything important.

All Lucia had known with any certainty was that the other witches hadn't given up the search for her leader, and she'd taken great pleasure in keeping his identity secret even when Pythia had offered a tamer sentence in exchange for a name. Just a name.

Her savior spilled her out of a black, lightweight sack into the middle of a glyph meant for reversing transformation spells. She blinked up at her master to find him as handsome as ever, his chiseled jawline surrounded by dozens of neat, tidy dreadlocks hanging past his broad shoulders. Darrell had played football in college and retained the athletic frame, his career as a construction worker no doubt coming into play.

He wore multiple chains around his neck, each one serving the same purposes as a witch's bangles and magical rings. As he pinched one gold strand between his fingers, the warlock placed the other hand atop her furry head.

Even though they were both self-taught, he had the affinity for the magical arts and enchantments Lucia lacked. All her talents were with potions and brewing.

All at once, power buzzed through her body on an electric current, tingling down to the tips of her delicate extremities. One moment, she flopped on the ground as a helpless bat, and in the next, she struggled to raise her human body onto her hands and knees. Close to a year of life as a bat had weakened her, and the smell of her animal form had been infused into her skin. She'd loathed that body, but the bat spirit had been the only creature willing to come to her back when she'd undergone the ritual to find an animal shape.

Then she'd lost her transformation bangle on Halloween night while fighting with River and Zacarias. Instead of giving it back to her, the Circle of Seven had decided leaving her in that flea-bitten shape was a just punishment.

"You came for me," she breathed, overcome with appreciation. A few tufts of bat fur still clung against her grimy arms as the gradual transformation took place. Unlike a true shapeshifter, reversing the spell restored Lucia's human body with her clothes intact.

"Did you think for a moment I'd leave you behind?"

She had, but she didn't dare admit it. Instead, she looked around and tried to make sense of her surroundings. Everything looked clean and fresh. Brand-new. The few pieces of furniture were all small, but equally as pristine.

"Where are we?" she asked him.

"A safe enough place where they can't find us," Darrell replied. He nodded toward the open doorway, the tile of a bathroom visible beyond it. Lucia could have wept in joy. "Go ahead and take your time. I got all your favorites stocked."

"In a moment."

Darrell smirked. "Want me to carry you in?"

"I can do it," she bit out. Her legs protested bearing her weight, but she flushed with triumph once she brought her trembling knees under control.

"I'll get some food while you get cleaned up. Thai still good for you?"

"Anything that doesn't involve fruit." She shuddered.

"Meat it is. I'll get you a variety."

Once he left, she abandoned the living room and stripped off her stinking clothes. All she wanted to do was incinerate them, but the topaz ring on her right hand fizzled when she tried to draw on the magic she had stored within. Either the witch had done something, or her time as a bat had depleted the energies. Replenishing her enchantments would be yet another thing to rectify.

She'd nearly forgotten how heavenly a scalding hot shower could be, and she lingered until the water began to run cold. As promised, the master had supplied all her favorite soaps and oils. Wrapped in a towel, she finished the rest of her beauty routine then wandered from the bathroom to explore the rest of the house. Inside a nearby bedroom, she found a selection from her personal closet. Darrell must have visited her apartment in San Antonio, and she appreciated the gesture.

But she loathed how the clothes hung loosely on her thinner frame. Months as a bat had been hell on her body, and she'd lost lean muscle and a little fat where it counted most.

By the time Darrell returned with food, she felt human again and had settled on the sofa with a candle to work on recharging her spells.

"You look better," he said.

"I feel better, thank you." Her belly made a loud noise as Darrel set out several white takeout cartons on the coffee table. A sharp, curt gesture of his hand bid Lucia to help herself, and she set aside her questions to satisfy her immediate hunger first.

Only when she'd cleared her first servings and drained a tall cup of water did she turn her mind back to everything she wanted to know. "How long was I held?"

"About eight months," he replied. "But don't worry, I made her pay for what she did to you. She won't be bothering anyone anymore."

"Good." She stabbed a tender morsel and popped it in her mouth. "What about Zacarias?"

"Shacked up with River. They've been living together since May. Like, living together, not just sharing a building." He portioned out more cashew chicken onto her plate. "You may as well give him up as a lost cause. He's proposing to her."

"I have no intentions of trying to get him back. Not anymore."

"Good. I don't need your personal life interfering with what I have set up here." He fixed her with a hard look. "Your bullshit addiction to him got you busted once. Don't let it happen again."

"It won't," Lucia said stiffly.

"I could have used you all of this time. I had to delay my plans and find a new way to acquire the energy we need for our revenge."

"The Blood Sacrament. I heard the witch discussing it."

He nodded and opened a beer can. "The power vacuum is complete. With it, we can funnel energy on a whim and siphon all the magic we need to make up for the years we've been denied adequate teaching. We'll be stronger than *all* of them."

"Will you be calling in the others?" she asked.

"No, not for this. They served their use during the ceremony, so I've sent them ahead to El Paso," Darrell replied. "The property up there will serve as a good base camp before we head west to deal with the Daughters of the Sun."

"Good," she mumbled around a mouthful of lo mein. "I'm ready to leave this godforsaken state behind. What about the vampires?"

Darrell chuckled. "They have their own agenda, but they've proven to be valuable for certain jobs. They may be inept as fuck, but it's all added to the chaos and kept the shifters busy chasing their own tails. They don't know where to turn."

"When do we move forward with the plan?"

"It's already in motion. By taking out Pythia, we've removed the most powerful witch in the immediate area. And thanks to the raid on your house last October, I have the names of the other council hags. Digging up their addresses took some work, but I have locations for two of them."

He may as well have given her an early Christmas present. The only thing that would be sweeter would be when they took River Jackson down for her meddling interference. Darrell had been content to leave River be before, but she was sure if she worked her influence over him, it wouldn't take much effort to sway the stronger warlock into seeing things *her* way.

CHAPTER 16

Hospitals were on River's list of places she least liked to visit. She never knew what to do and loathed standing in the sterile, impersonal corridors and rooms reeking of medicinal products or sickness.

But she set those misgivings aside to stop in and check on Pythia. No matter what the woman had done, no matter what she had hidden away and kept secret, she hadn't deserved what Darrell had done to her and her home.

Expecting the worst, River stepped into the room and faced her former mentor. Pythia lay upon the narrow hospital bed in traction, one leg snapped at the shin and set with pins in some gruesome looking torture device. The left arm had a hard cast, and ugly purple bruises stained her upper chest and shoulders, visible above the neckline of a white and blue hospital gown.

River blinked away the tears. It had been three days since Darrell had almost murdered Pythia, and they weren't any closer to tracking him down. Meanwhile, the insidious pulse of something terrible loomed over the town like storm clouds preparing to unleash a torrent of despair.

No matter how much she wanted to hate Pythia for manipulating and using her, the sight of her fragile and broken body in the hospital bed tempered River's resentment.

"River…"

Her gaze snapped away from the lifted leg to Pythia's pale face. "Hey… I, um, brought some crystals for you."

She held up the potted echinacea flowers she'd brought. Beads of amber, jasper, hematite, and turquoise strung on copper wire had been wrapped around the ceramic pot. The pretty pink, purple, and yellow flowers added some much needed color to the otherwise plain room.

"You didn't need to do that."

"I did," River said. "We didn't part on the best of terms, and this is the least I can do."

The brief, fragile smile on Pythia's face tugged at her heartstrings. "That was my fault. Not yours. But I am glad you came, River. I… I am so sorry."

"I know," River replied in a low voice. She set the pot down on the bedside table and took a seat in the provided chair. "Are they treating you all right?"

"As best they can. Food isn't so good."

"Is it ever?" River laughed and ducked her head. "Lucia's gone. He took her."

Pythia released a long sigh and closed her eyes. "I thought that might be the case."

"Can you tell me what happened?"

"It all happened so fast. I didn't even sense his approach. He took down my wards before I even knew what was happening."

"What?" River doubted in her own abilities to deal with the magical protections Pythia had in place. They were among the strongest she'd ever encountered.

"That's not all." Pythia's hand shook as it lifted from the sheets. She reached out and River took the older woman's hand in her own. "He took my powers. I can't use them anymore."

If she hadn't been sitting already, she might have fallen. Pythia's words seemed to sweep the floor out from beneath her feet, making her go dizzy. "I don't understand. What do you mean you can't use your powers?"

"He took them," Pythia said in a trembling voice. "My powers are gone. I can't feel my attunement to the world of magic anymore. I can't sense the darkness or anything amiss. I can't even enjoy the healing vibrations your gift was meant to deliver. There's only an enormous void there now."

"But how?"

"His talisman. He wears one around his neck, much like the one we confiscated from Lucia."

"The one in her car," River whispered. "I'd seen it at least a half dozen times before whenever she'd come by to bug Zac, but I never really *saw* it. Didn't pay it any attention. Something about it diverted my attention elsewhere."

Of course, she'd also been distracted by trying to save Zacarias from his ex.

River's shoulders fell, and before she could excuse herself to allow Pythia to rest, a sharp rap on the door and a friendly greeting announced Rhona's arrival. The elderly witch stepped inside, bearing a similar offering designed to expedite Pythia's recovery.

"So, judging from your solemn expressions, I sense that I've arrived at a tense moment," Rhona said carefully. "Is this a poor time to share the fruit of my investigation, or would you both like to hear what I've discovered recently."

"Please share it," Pythia implored.

"Let me begin by stating I would have had this to you sooner had it not been necessary to probe through two decades of data." Rhona unsnapped the leather bag on her lap and removed a slim manila folder. "This is from the Archives of the Gifted in Austin where we keep record of every magical child we encounter. Other states did it differently back then. Of course, we've now moved to an online database, but most of the file hasn't been transcribed."

River took the folder and opened it to reveal a handwritten sheet of parchment in elongated, flowing script. As she skimmed the contents, her brows drew close together.

At the Crone's behest, I have interviewed the father of Darrell Tyler at length and discussed the many incidents of grave concern that led him to my office. Unexplainable events in the home implicate unhoned magical ability, however, the child was unable or unwilling to replicate these effects in my presence. The mother is a deceased member of our sisterhood, and had she undertaken the initial stages of his education, he may have developed a greater potential for magic. As it stands, I am unwilling to invest the time in nurturing her progeny's meager talents.

As males often make unscrupulous and equally unsatisfactory witches, I have chosen at this time to deny the father's request and no formal training shall occur. Perhaps in five or ten years, I may revisit this decision. It is most probable his attunement to the magical world will atrophy and shrivel.

River squeezed the sheet hard enough to crease it. "So he was turned away. For nothing more than being a boy."

Pythia closed her eyes, appearing pale and fragile against the stark white sheets. "It was a different time then. Harsher. Boys were still frowned upon by many in the order, despite having the same talents. Those who were… uncooperative were often passed over."

Rhona dipped her head and frowned. "Perhaps this is why he's targeting us."

"It doesn't excuse the path he's taken. Not at all. Not even a little, but I've never felt shame like this before," River said. "Secrets, outright *betrayal*, and turning aside people needing our help. What, he was a little shy during the interview so she decided he wasn't worth teaching? He was probably scared. I was petrified the first time Mom brought me to meet the other witches."

But they'd welcomed her with open arms and plied her with gifts of unusual worth. Now she knew why, and it boiled her blood the more she thought about it. Had they been sucking up to her? Hoping to ingratiate themselves in her presence so that when she later awakened her powers, they'd have a goddess in their pocket.

River glanced down at the paper again, mouth pressed into a tight line when she saw the name of the registrar who turned Darrell away. Grace. One of the oldest among the Texas witches, and also, from what River had gathered last year, the most impatient.

"There's nothing to be done about it now," Pythia said. She reached over with her fragile, uninjured hand and touched River's arm. "But you're right that it doesn't excuse his behavior now. He had a choice. He chose to become a murderer to teach us a lesson."

"He must be stopped, no matter what. But how do we stop a man who has the ability to steal our gifts from us?" Rhona asked, revealing she'd already learned the grim news.

Chilled by the bleak possibility, River shivered. "I don't know. All I can say with any certainty is he's a danger to every witch he encounters until we can find and stop him."

And if he'd stolen the powers of the most powerful witch River knew, how the hell was she supposed to have a chance at stopping him? They might have thought she had the soul of a goddess inside her, but potential didn't equate to skill.

If anything, her unique gift made her more of a target.

***

When all other methods failed to locate Darrell, River tried scrying. She held her divining charm above a map of

Texas and infused the slender shard of moonstone with enough magic to push it into a slow and rhythmic rotation. It spun and spun above the map, gradually moving off center and occasionally tightening into a smaller circle above the San Antonio area. It widened again, repeating that pattern for several minutes.

Inconclusive. Damn. Learning nothing more than what she already knew about his whereabouts, she stuffed the crystal back into her drawer and sank down onto the pile of cushions on the floor of her meditation room.

What the hell kind of goddess did they believe her to be if she couldn't even locate an evil dark witch? Trembling with resentment, she raked her fingers through her wild curls and tried to get herself together.

How the hell was she supposed to accomplish what Texas's best witches failed to do? Aside from that, she'd received another call from her father with veiled insinuations about her and Zac legitimizing their living arrangements. Her paternal grandparents wanted to know when they'd have *kids*. Kids weren't even a blip on River's radar.

Everyone had wants, but River's greatest desire of the moment would have been to cuddle beside Zac in bed while he stretched alongside her in his panther form. She wanted to run her fingers through his ebony coat and feel the rumbles of his purring beneath her cheek.

Zacarias peeked inside, leading her to wonder if he could read minds. "Safe to come in?"

The meditation room had become one of those places where Zacarias didn't bother or interrupt her, not that her sweetheart ever truly bothered her. He'd simply told her that he recognized once she settled on the cushions, she was there to attain a need he couldn't provide: peace.

"Yeah. Come on. I told you, you're welcome to come inside any time I'm in here." She beckoned him with both hands until he padded barefoot to the edge of the soft mats.

"Everyone's going to bed early. All this searching and tracking across the town has them beat. Ian said he's never flown so much in his... Hey? Are you all right?"

She forced a thin smile onto her face. "Just thinking."

"About?" he asked, lowering to join her on the floor. He took both of her hands and held them in his warm grip, smoothing a thumb over the back of her knuckles.

"Everything that's happening. Everything that has to be done, and the big mess Darrell has made of everything. I didn't think I could ever hate someone so much, and I'm angry at myself for letting it fester in my heart. Hate isn't what I'm supposed to be about."

"It's a valid human emotion, Riv... It's okay to feel angry, and it's okay to hate him for what he did." His thumb continued to stroke over the back of her hand, sweeping back and forth. "He did an awful thing to two people you care about. What matters is letting it go before it consumes you though. Because you're better than him, and he's not worthy of your attention like that. Get what I'm saying?"

She nodded quietly. Try as she might to hold it back, the first tear fell, creating a slick path down her left cheek. Her right eye blurred and trickled over too.

Zac held her, without judgment or further words, he held her closely in those impossibly strong arms she'd come to rely on. And when her tears ended, he wiped her cheeks, sweeping his thumbs beneath her eyes and drying her face. "All better?"

"Yeah... I think so." She managed to smile.

"Good. I kinda came up to talk to you about something big. And private."

He glanced toward the door, like he wished he'd closed it. River gestured with her right hand, activating the energy ring she used for telekinetic force. The door drifted shut and clicked into place. And then he removed a simple black box from his jeans.

"Zac..."

"This isn't the real one," he began, as he flipped up the lid, "because the one I truly want to give you belonged to my grandmother."

Startled enough to jump up to her feet, River held both hands to her mouth and stared down at what had to be one of the most beautiful stones she'd ever seen. It wasn't a diamond—Zac knew her better than to provide her with an impersonal stone like that—but it shone up at her in two of her favorite colors. The purple and green looked good against the sterling silver band. "It's... it's so pretty."

"It's ruby in zoisite," he explained in a soft voice, any quieter and she'd have to strain to hear him. "It would mean a lot to me if you wore my grandmother's old ring, but... I also wanted to give you this. To protect you."

Every ring on her fingers had meaning and a purpose, none of them worn simply for aesthetics and show.

Painstaking hours had imbued each one with different enchantments meant to augment her magic, store spells, or provide some sort of benefit.

"I don't know if…"

"The very kind witch who sold me the raw stone said it's for protection from storms, warding off negativity, and courage."

"And passion," she murmured.

"And passion, not that you need help with either of the last two. You are courage personified, Riv, and there could be no higher honor for me than if you'd consent to be my wife."

Her gaze dropped to the ring again as she nibbled her lower lip. "I don't know if I can be the kind of wife you deserve. My life is always going to be hectic, and busy, and strange, and full of shit happening that's going to get in between us. Because I can't step back and away from things now."

Her boyfriend blinked up at her, still holding his pose on the floor at her feet. "I don't understand."

"There's something I haven't told you." Hell, there were a lot of somethings she hadn't told him, but one in particular seemed worse than the others, the kind of dishonesty he didn't deserve. "When I argued with Pythia, it was about more than her refusing to help and putting me through the wringer."

"What is it, *querida*? You can tell me anything."

"Pythia says I'm not a witch."

"So last Halloween those weren't spells you were slinging around?" His puzzled expression shifted into a mischievous grin, humor shining in his eyes. "What are you then? A Jedi? That could be sorta sexy."

His inherent geekiness was one of the many things she loved about him, and she wished she could laugh along and claim that she wielded the Force. "No, not a Jedi." She wished it could be that simple, because maybe fighting Imperials on the big screen would be easier than battling dark witches and powerful warlocks in the shadows.

"Then what?"

"She and the other two think I'm... one of the goddesses of magic, reborn into flesh."

He blinked, and any other time she would have found his owlish expression adorable. "Come again?"

"They believe I am the reincarnation of the goddess Circe."

"Circe? As in the Greek chick who turned guys into pigs?"

She really hoped that part of the myth was an exaggeration. "Yes, more or less. And the truth is, I actually believe she means it. It's the only thing that explains how I've been able to do the things I can. Things no normal witch can."

"I don't care," he said after a quiet moment of studying her.

"It's easy to say now, but months, or maybe even years from now, you'll feel differently. I'm not... I'm not a normal person anymore."

"No, you certainly aren't." Her shoulders fell after he voiced his agreement. Zac pushed to his feet and set his hands on her hips. "You're my River. Normal isn't a thing

I ever saw in you, not once since the first day we met. I don't give a damn what you are, whether it's human, witch, or… or a goddess, because I fell in love with *you* for who you are. Not the things you can do."

Stinging tears welled over her lashes and coursed down her cheeks in hot trails before she could hold them back. "I don't deserve you. How did I end up with such a great guy?"

His smile softened as he wiped away her fresh tears. "You helped me wash my car in those ridiculously short shorts, and I don't think there's a straight man alive who could resist you when you're strutting around like that. I decided right then you had to be mine."

She swatted his chest.

"What? I mean it. Every word I said is true. I'm always going to be in your corner. If at any time you felt I wasn't there for you through this, then I'm sorry." His lips traced the curve of her shoulder, abrading her skin with his unshaven cheek. That always gave her goose bumps and sent little shivers down her spine.

"No, it's not that," she assured him, although she dragged in a ragged breath afterward. "I just…" At a loss for words, she fell silent for a while before blurting, "I love you."

Zac dropped the box aside on the hardwood floor beside the mats. The cold metal ring slid onto her finger. "I love you, and I want to spend my life with you. And there's something else."

"What?"

"Ever since the day we met, I've wanted to claim you as mine. My panther recognized you as my mate before I did. That's something Lucia and I never shared."

"You mean you two never…?" Despite dating a shifter and living alongside him day to day, River had a woefully inadequate knowledge of their culture. Realizing that now, she gulped down another sob borne from her failures related to their relationship. How could she have stretched herself so thin?

"Bonded? No. We didn't. I never felt the compulsion, and I guess it's a good thing, or I wouldn't be here with you now to tell you how much I love you."

"And how do you feel with me?"

"Every damned day is a struggle, fighting to hold back natural instinct, but not wanting to force it on you in a moment of passion. I wanted it to be something *we* decided. Together. You get what I mean?"

"I'd be a fool if I said no."

"Whether you say yes or no, I'll love you no less, and weeks from now—no, months or even years from now, I'll still be waiting for you to say yes. I won't change my mind. You won't run me off."

"And my duties?"

"They can't chase me away either. As long as you always do what you think is right, I'll be right here beside you."

Her breath quickened, one trace of his fingertips beneath her loose shirt enough to kick her heart rhythm into hyperdrive. Both of his hands skimmed over her ribs and peeled the plain cotton tee over her head. "And if we bond, what does that mean? Is it really like... sharing a soul?"

"For us, bonding is as intimate as it gets, *querida*. Yeah. I give you a little piece of me, and I guess I get a tiny piece of you."

The unspoken question hung between them: if she was a goddess as the Trinity believed, what the hell would Zac receive in return?

"Let's do it."

Without a need for more words or persuasion, Zac lowered her to the pillows scattered across the floor. Silk cushions in an assortment of warm colors supported her naked back, and he slid one bent knee between her thighs while he dipped down to lay a path of kisses from her shoulder to her breasts. Each light touch was like the brush of butterfly wings against her flushed skin, tender and fleeting.

"Zac," River moaned, arching her back from the cushions in an attempt to find firmer contact. When he laughed, his warm breath feathered across her skin.

"In a rush?"

"Rushing is an understatement. I'm dying to have you touch me." Because it had been too long, the ongoing peril of chasing a warlock dousing their passion with ice water.

"Patience, my goddess. Good things to those who wait."

His goddess? She hadn't thought there were sexier words than when Zac spoke to her in his native language, but he proved her wrong. He drew out her sweet torture, leaving a trail of scorching kisses and maddening nibbles down the length of her body until he lowered his face between her legs and took his first taste. River grasped a handful of dark hair in one hand and gripped one of his muscled shoulders with the other.

With only a few laps of his tongue and glides of his talented fingers, he brought her to a state of overwhelming ecstasy. Not once, but twice, he arrested all movement when she reached the precipice, only to begin the frustrating pattern anew. Finally, when she could take no more and wept for relief, he thrust her over the edge by sealing his lips where it mattered most.

By the time Zac raised his head, his green eyes smoldered with insurmountable desire and left no doubt about his mutual need. While she trembled, pleasure coursing through her in shimmering waves, her lover stretched himself above the curves he'd tenderly undressed and joined their bodies.

"I am forever yours, River," he whispered against her cheek. "If you'll have me."

Forever could be a long time for a witch, and even longer for a goddess, but no matter the stance she took, there was nothing River wanted more. "Yes," she cried as the next thrust rocked her body. She searched desperately for anything to grab, but discovered only pillows and the chiseled body atop her. With a handful of satin cushion in her left hand, she wrapped the other around his nape and arched her hips from the floor. "Yours. Always yours."

Her chest swelled with too much love to be contained by one heart, and for a moment, she was his helpless captive, trembling beneath him as another climax thrust her into ecstasy. Endless pleasure became an infinite loop of give and take, Zac's desperation to join her in orgasm felt in the frenzied rhythm of his strokes.

A low growl rumbled in Zac's chest, the sexiest sound she'd ever heard from him. He withdrew and rolled River onto her side before framing her body with his brawny biceps. Something about him, whether it was his hungry stare or the rumbling purr in his chest, seemed more feral than usual. As if she'd surrendered to the beast inside him.

He bowed over her body, and then the sharp pinch of his teeth seized the back of her neck from behind. The bite lasted only seconds, long enough to place an irreversible claim upon her soul. Whether it was normal for shifter mates or because she was a witch—greater than a witch—the distinct power of their blooming bond washed over her in golden waves until she was molten with pleasure. They breathed as one, bodies tuning to each other in a matched rhythm.

And every second was bliss. Perspiration dotted Zac's brow and his beautiful green and gold eyes shone, lit from behind and shimmering brightly.

In the glowing aftermath, they held each other close, arms and legs tangled together. She dreaded what tomorrow would bring, so for now, she cast it from her mind and focused on the moment. *Their* moment.

"Does this mean we're married now?"

Zac nuzzled her throat and nipped the sensitive skin over her beating pulse. "As far as shifters are concerned? Yeah. But I still wanna give you a wedding with our families present. Make it all legal so your pops won't grumble at me anymore."

She closed her eyes and smiled. "How about we elope after we get back from Brazil?"

"If that's what you want." He made a soft sound reminiscent of a purr and snuggled in closer. His breaths evened out and his heartbeat slowed to a soothing, sedate pace. Of course, the first snore ruined the peaceful interlude, and she laughed quietly to herself.

Mine, River thought fiercely as the peaceful rhythm of his heart carried her to sleep.

CHAPTER 17

Zacarias peered out the window and down the residential road. Usually, he saw kids in the distance playing ball beneath the street lamps, but the curfew had transformed Atropos into a ghost town after dark. There hadn't been wandering groups of teens or late evening horseback riders since Pam and Jack's murder, and there weren't many adults out either in even the populated neighborhoods. Since the highway weaved through their little community and most travelers happily blew through without stopping on their way to San Antonio, businesses who thrived on evening activity from teens were reeling from the curfew.

The owners of the local fast food chains had applied enough pressure to Mayor Johnson for the man to reconsider it. During the summer, they counted on teens piling into their businesses to buy hamburgers and pizzas.

Dusty had called less than an hour ago with a plea for River to work faster. He didn't know if he could get the mayor to hold on much longer before lifting it.

Outside, the wind whipped through the trees and bent some of the smaller saplings in their yard until their slender trunks nearly touched the ground. Energy charged the air, and the enormous blood-red moon hung in the black, starless sky.

Using her favorite deck of Oracle cards, River had attempted to perform a second divining ritual to locate Darrell, using harmless belongings from his apartment as her focus, but all she'd turned up from the reading was that he was somewhere isolated and distant from other people, and of course, alone save for the dark witch's presence.

Alone made Zacarias think the woods or forest, perhaps even the nearby camping ground preferred by the local Boy Scout troop, but they had already raced there and confirmed it was empty.

Ian hadn't yet returned from an evening hunt with the werewolves, and Lyle was conserving his strength, almost recovered from his injuries. Despite two wolf packs and two pairs of avian eyes above Atropos and its neighboring area, they still hadn't found anything.

"Something is going to happen tonight," River said, pacing a groove in the floor. She'd been up and walking for over thirty minutes, too agitated to remain still. "I don't feel like I'm doing enough. I don't know *what* to do. What good is being a goddess if I'm helpless?"

Zacarias caught her on the next circuit before she could wear the new floor rug thin. "You're not helpless. This is the panic talking." He held her by the shoulders and stooped to her eye level. "I know you feel like you're running out of time, but this isn't your fault."

He'd watched her torture herself over her inability to find Darrell, a witch who, for all intents and purposes, shouldn't have a fraction of her powers, but he'd been the helpless one, unable to provide anything more than moral support and unwelcomed protection.

After all, when he had been needed, he hadn't been there, away on a stupid business meeting when Maiara accompanied her to question vampires. Finding her comatose on the couch had been one of his worst nightmares.

"It *is* my fault. If I was better, I'd be able to pinpoint his location. I'd be able to say more than the obvious."

Zac wanted to shake her, but he resisted, squeezing her shoulders instead and gazing into her hazel eyes. "No," he said gently.

"But—"

"No." After sternly repeating himself, he smoothed his hands up and down her arms. "What did I tell you about blaming and doubting yourself? Stop and breathe, River. Calm down and let the thoughts come to you. Remember how you told me inspiration sometimes comes to you on its own? Then let it. Clear your mind."

"Clear my mind," she murmured. She'd appeared mildly insulted at first, wrinkling her brow at him and pursing her lips, but her tensed shoulders loosened.

Maiara set aside her book and gazed up at them. "He is correct," the bear shifter said before rising to her feet to stretch. "Let it come to you. Should we visit your special room?"

He hadn't seen River in her meditation room in the couple days since their bonding, and he had to wonder if it was a source of motivation for her, his witch often struck by strange moments of insight long after she'd relaxed. Except for that night.

"You're both right," River murmured. Her shoulders dipped. "I guess I thought I could stress myself into providing results. Everyone's counting on me."

"They are, but we all understand you aren't a machine that can churn out ideas on a whim. We're all stumped, baby."

After taking her hand, Zac tugged his fiancée upstairs, settled her in the meditation room, poured her a glass of wine, and played the role of the dutiful mate by kneading the soles of her bare feet. He worked in silence, refusing to shatter the illusion of peace while she lay sprawled on her back.

If it was guaranteed to do more for her nerves than his pleasure, he would have coaxed her out of her clothing and rubbed her back too.

Zac was still debating the merit of it when River jerked upright and yanked her foot from his hands to blurt out, "This is the night of the Lughnasadh."

"The what?" Zac asked, bewildered by her outburst.

"It's a Pagan holiday."

"Okay, but what's that got to do with anything?"

"There's power in dates, I mean, not the date itself, but in the activities that take place. On any day when hundreds or thousands of people gather for a common goal, there's going to be a surge of power. Many members of our sisterhood also join festivals thrown during Lammas. It's a time of reflection dedicated to the Sun God, Lugh, and also a period to celebrate... to celebrate the harvest." She raised a hand to her mouth and stared with wide eyes through the windows.

"River?"

She bolted out of the room and down the stairs with Zac hot on her heels. She didn't stop until she reached the cell phone she'd left on the coffee table and swept it off the glossy surface. As Maiara blinked at her in alarm, she jabbed a name on the contact list. "He's perverting the holiday to do something awful."

"To do what?" Zacarias asked.

River didn't answer him. The other participant of the conversation must have picked up the line, because she began repeating the same speech without a greeting or hello.

Now she was speaking a mile a minute, her eyes all aglow with energy and fervor he hadn't seen before. Lyle hadn't stirred once, the insensible dog shifter sprawled on his back on the couch. On the other love seat, Maiara leaned forward with interest, muscles tensed to rise.

"Is it time to battle the warlock?" she asked, eagerness shining in her brown eyes.

"It may be. But we still don't have a location. I mean, we've checked everywhere. We even drove to his dad's house out in Austin to check on him. Harrison got into his bank and credit accounts, so we're positive he's paying cash anywhere he goes."

"And hotels?"

"Under another name and face *if* he's even using one at all. He's thought of everything," Zacarias muttered. "We were optimistic enough to hope he'd left clues behind at his job, but the foreman at the construction site said Darrell walked off the job and stopped showing up for work over a week ago. Then another of their guys went missing and... That's it!"

Lyle startled awake this time and almost flopped off the couch. "What's what? What's happening, huh?" The drowsy coonhound rubbed both eyes and blearily glanced around the room.

River peeked over from her phone call. "What?"

"I think I know where we can find Darrell," Zacarias said. "Okay, he's got this big construction gig working for his uncle, right? Some company bought up a bunch of land to build identical, overpriced houses on the outskirts of Atropos. Lots of money involved. We've been looking for him at hotels and checking in with friends, but with his face splashed all over the news, who needs to get a hotel when you have rows of newly constructed houses to hide out in."

"Then we need to get over there," Lyle said. "I'll make the calls to Ian and Argus. You handle whatever you need for us to hit the road and get moving."

***

The wind whipped River's hair around her face, blowing through the empty development with an eerie howl. Tommy and Argus had brought plenty of wolves, piling their four-legged packmates into the beds of two different trucks before meeting them on the outskirts of town. Zac and River had caught a ride with Ian in his SUV, and she'd been startled by how cool and collected he appeared, like a badass who belonged on the set of *The Expendables*, while armed with a glowing water gun.

"Was I right?" Zac asked.

River took a few steps down the road and raised her face toward the sky. "The air is volatile here... I'd be surprised if you were wrong."

When some firm had purchased the land just outside of Atropos city limits, she'd had her doubts about whether the project would ever get finished. It had been plagued by all kinds of bad luck and two guys had even died in the early days—a senseless accident with no one to blame but the deceased, according to the *Atropos Daily*. A lot of palms had been greased when it should have been shut down, but Darrell's uncle had been able to prove it was by no negligence of their workers. Just a couple of irresponsible tradesmen and plain bad luck.

Then there'd been another member of the crew who went missing only two weeks ago. Thinking back on all the drama that had taken place and comparing it against the knowledge of Darrell's monstrous activities, River had no doubts about what happened to those men.

Darrell had used them, and she'd never even noticed.

Not my fault, River reminded herself. Zacarias and Maiara were right on that front. How could she be responsible for every magical crime that occurred across the state, or even in her own town?

Pausing in the middle of a street bordered by heavy construction equipment, she tilted her face toward the sky and closed her eyes. Unseen motes of energy sparked against her skin, falling like ethereal kisses in the dark. The sharp and sweet taste of magic circulated through the charged air.

"It's a spell," she whispered. "We have to stop him before he can complete the spell."

"What about the other witches?"

"I told them where to come, but we don't have time to waste. This is happening *now*."

River had donned her favorite corset, which she'd affectionately dubbed her good-luck bustier since it had gotten her through a battle with Lucia nine months ago. All she'd added since then was a bandolier across her chest equipped with several bottles of liquid sunshine.

"Then we will help you end it," Maiara said.

"Damn straight," Tommy agreed.

River looked between the faces of all her friends and gave a quick nod. They could do this. They *had* to do this.

"Stay sharp, everyone. There's no telling what we'll be facing," Ian called out.

"Vampires," River said in a low voice. "I can feel them."

She recognized the same feeling from the house when she'd found Bobby, an uncomfortable itch in her mind and a slow, cold trickle down her spine.

"You sure? I can't smell anything over all this magic in the air," Lyle said.

"Yeah," she replied. "I am."

"Good enough for me," Ian said. "All right, everyone, our job is to provide support to River and keep the vamps off her tail. If you see the warlock, do not engage. Leave it to her."

"Agreed," Tommy said. "We'll split up and scout ahead. If one of us howls, we've found him."

She flashed him a grateful smile. "Thank you."

Coached by Ian and Argus, the group of wolves fanned out over the surroundings to cover more ground while River and Zacarias prowled ahead. With magical force all abuzz in the air, Darrell had hampered her ability to pinpoint any one location.

He could have been anywhere. The knowledge chilled her, raising goose bumps on her bare arms.

"Vampires at ten o'clock," Harrison called out. A wolf barreled past them, stirring the air again.

"And on our six," Ian replied. After he executed a perfect shot, golden beams lit up the night with the brilliant warmth of the sun. A vampire's high-pitched shriek strained River's eardrums, and flames sparked across its blistering skin. With the next shot from Harrison, it combusted from head to toe.

Half a dozen slunk out from the completed houses, fangs bared, but River sensed more in the shadows lurking and waiting, likely opportunistic predators waiting for them to run low on potion.

If this wasn't proof of the vampires working alongside Darrell, then nothing would satisfy the Council of Seven. Not that she cared about meeting their demands for proof anymore. From now on, they were going to do things her way or risk losing her forever.

The vampires moved fast, rushing in without any sense of caution. She'd bet anything they were recently turned. Something about the feral, hungry gleam in their eyes betrayed they didn't have the patience born from centuries of life.

Light exploded to her left as a sunlight vial shattered against the paved road. The recoiling vampires shrieked and shrank away from the attack. Wisps of smoke trailed toward the sky, visible in the beams of yellow light created by her alchemical concoction.

Upon whirling to see who had lobbed the vial, River found herself staring at the flashing red and blue of police lights. "*Dusty?*"

Another white SUV pulled up bearing the Atropos Police Department logo. "Clark and the others are back in the town holding it down for us," Dusty called out to her from the driver's side.

"You don't have to help. This isn't your fight."

"Yeah, but y'all can't ever say we don't take care of our own. The job's to serve and protect, ma'am," Officer Morales said. "It doesn't differentiate between vampires and normal criminals."

"Okay. Stay back here and help keep them off us."

In the distance, directly before them and to the left, a wolf's lone howl pierced the night. The fine hairs on the back of River's neck rose, and she shivered despite knowing the shifter was on their side.

"Go on, you two," Ian encouraged with a wave of his hand. "We'll help Dusty handle the leeches. You get Darrell."

"Be careful," Zac said before he dove from two legs to four. River took a vial in hand then sprinted off with her panther at her side. Her feet pounded against fresh asphalt, and her lungs burned for air as she dashed around the corner onto the next lane of the planned community. The magic radiating from the construction project washed against her senses like an oily wave.

They left finished homes behind and entered an area with uncompleted buildings. The skeletal frames of a few two-story buildings had been erected on concrete slabs.

Two figures in dark clothes stood at opposite sides of a power circle drawn onto a large, empty foundation. Fat candles outlined the perimeter, their wicks tipped by green flames. Every step closer increased River's apprehension, until she had to physically lean forward and push through the repulsion. Beside her, Zac growled.

"We have company," Lucia said. She tossed her hair back over her shoulder and stared River down. "Shall I deal with them, Master?"

"Darrell, you have to stop this," River yelled.

He flicked his fingers toward them in response, releasing a powerful blast. River threw her arms out in front of her and shielded against the raw energy. The saplings to her right didn't fare as well. The thin trunks snapped in half and every leaf ripped off like a child blowing on a dandelion puff.

"Have at your ex, Lucia. River is mine."

"With pleasure."

Darrell's watch flared red seconds before a fiery jet rushed toward River. She batted the flames aside and countered with a fireball drawn from her flame ring. Her bracelets danced and jangled over her wrists, singing with defensive power.

For every attack Darrell sent her way, she blocked or countered, pushing him further and further away from the circle. From the corners of her eyes, she caught fleeting glimpses of Zac and Lucia. So far, the panther was quick enough to keep ahead of his ex-wife, but he hadn't managed to take her down, and it was only a matter of time before the witch broke through his defenses.

Zac's incredible shifter speed had overwhelmed Lucia before, but they'd also worked alongside each other and done it as a team.

A team. Golden light lit up the sky from the corner of River's peripheral vision. A vampire screamed in agonized wails. Somewhere out there, the rest of their friends were still alive.

"I gave you the chance to stay out of my business, River. I warned you."

Her gaze darted to the side to keep tabs on Zacarias and Lucia. Using a haste spell to expedite her retreat, the witch streaked away around the corner and out of sight, with the panther giving chase behind her. Dammit.

River cut her attention back to Darrell. "I don't handle warnings well."

Back before she and Zac had gotten serious, she'd met Darrell once or twice in passing through town. She'd even thought him handsome, the kind of guy her father would have wanted her to date.

Looking at him now, all she could see was Pam's murderer and the cold monster who had snuffed out Jack's life with the casual ease of exterminating a pest.

"I won't rest until I've ended your stupid fucking sisterhood," Darrell yelled across the turbulent field created by his defensive wards. "Witches—*all witches*—must be destroyed."

"That's crazy talk, and you know it," she countered. "I found out what happened to you, and I'm sorry you had to suffer all this time, but this isn't the way to fix things. You're hurting innocent people. You *murdered* people who had nothing to do with this!"

"Their sacrifice will benefit everyone."

"Sacrifice is never the path to take. It won't do you any good in the end, believe me."

"Shows how little you know."

Darrell and Lucia had created multiple layers of protection, erecting a barrier unlike anything she'd ever encountered in all her years as Pythia's pupil. With each ring she surpassed, she discovered another stronger barrier beneath it, charged with a different magical trait.

"River," Gloria cried from the outskirts of the magical field. "We're here to help."

One by one, the most powerful and experienced witches in all of Texas approached the concrete slab, each one holding her preferred tool or method of casting spells. They ranged in physical ages, a handful as young as Gloria and River, while others ran the gamut to their senior years.

And every single one had lived multiple lifetimes.

Relief coursed through River when she felt their magic push against the gloom. She wasn't alone, after all. They hadn't sent her forward to fight Darrell like a lamb for the slaughter. "You can't win here."

"Oh, yeah? You did exactly what I wanted you to do," Darrell cried in triumph, raising both of his fists toward the sky. The miasma whipping around the concrete slab picked up speed and suddenly swelled, reaching a dramatic crescendo that swept out until it reached each of the powerful witches originally standing beyond its perimeter. "Now all of your powers will belong to me."

Gloria screamed first, and then Daphne collapsed to her knees and clutched her head.

"No!" Grace lunged forward and threw out her hands, palms out. The three rings on her left hand blazed in scintillating hues of pink and purple, matched by the jeweled cuff bracelet on her right wrist. The resulting shockwave pushed Darrell back, though he managed to stay on his feet.

"You," he hissed, his eyes narrowing. "I remember you, you old bitch."

Quicker than a time-lapse video, multiple plants sprouted from the ground. As they twined and twisted together—an ability that could only be Pythia's stolen talent for garden magic—the bulk of the monstrosity snapped forward toward Grace. It wrapped around her frail body like an enormous green fist.

River's flame ring sputtered, exhausted of its remaining charges and incapable of conjuring another wisp of fire. Then the elder hit the wall with a sickening thump.

"Grace!" River cried out as the remaining vines entangled them all. Somewhere within her, a font of energy burst free. Despite the loss of her flame ring, heat danced around her in a wicked spiral, incinerating each plant without harming the women trapped inside them.

Claudia tried to run to their fellow sister, but she stumbled and collapsed halfway across the distance, crying out in the same manner as the others. Only River and Rhona remained standing, but a quick glance to her left showed Rhona's face pinched in pain and her hands shaking.

"Hold on, Rhona," River pleaded.

"I'm trying, but the pain…"

Blood dripped from Rhona's nose and her breaths quickened. Like the others before her, her magic sputtered and then fizzled out completely. The older witch's eyes rolled back in her head and she collapsed to the ground.

Darrell's smile faded. "Why isn't it working on you? I did the math. My calculations were correct."

"Because I'm not a witch."

"Whatever you are, you shouldn't have gotten in my way. I warned you. I didn't want to hurt you, but you forced this to happen. You asked for this." Lightning blazed down from the sky in a scintillating arc, exploding against the concrete. Several small chunks slapped against her body and face, drawing stinging lines of blood. Darrell displayed a strength she hadn't expected, but he was crude with his magic. Blunt.

"Just die!" Darrell screamed. He directed bolt after bolt at her, throwing them like a child having a tantrum. Cracks splintered across River's shield, but the mystic dome held beneath the assault.

Trash and debris left behind by the construction crew rose in the air, joined by some kind of mystical force. They flew together and became a moving, lethal wave that spiraled through the air and came crashing toward her.

The barrier didn't endure. It cracked beneath the force, and the final seconds of the onslaught ripped against River's skin and face, pummeling her hands and tearing ribbons of flesh from her palms. She screamed and stumbled to the side.

Darrell howled in triumph, the sound more animal than human. He spoke in a harsh, guttural language River didn't recognize. The sound grated against her ears and stabbed through her head.

A thunderous crack split the sky overhead, followed by an immediate flash. Darrell's sharp gestures seemed to guide the lightning, drawing it down and sending it straight at River's heart.

She caught the white-hot bolt three inches from her face. The power and energy crackled around her hand, but it didn't burn. Everything seemed to slow as she followed through with her body's momentum, turning in a full circle with the lightning bolt in hand, before releasing it. The brilliant lance flashed across the space between them and pierced Darrel's chest.

In that split second of time, the bolt given physical form highlighted his facial expression. The maniacal expression of triumph gave way to confusion, surprise, and finally pain. His lips formed a shocked circle as he staggered, and his gaze dropped to the smoking hole in his chest.

At the same time, a shockwave rippled outward in a circle, tearing through open space and down the streets. It tossed River back and off her feet, throwing her painfully onto her bottom on the hard ground then bouncing her head against the concrete slab. Startled, she bit her tongue, flooding her mouth with the taste of her own blood.

A brilliant rectangle of red erupted all at once at the edge of the cement, floating vertically above a circle drawn in what looked like drying blood. The crackling flames framed a terrifying window into impenetrable darkness and shadows.

A cold knot formed in the pit of River's belly. Then movement from the corner of her eye caught her attention as Lucia sprinted by her and snatched something from Darrell's corpse. Still dizzy from the strike to her head, River lurched to her feet and pulled magic from a fulgurite ring around her index finger, the polished bit of glass created when lightning struck sand. She hurled an electrical bolt across the space and missed the mark completely.

The questionable doorway disintegrated into cinders moments after Lucia darted through it.

River's frantic thoughts turned to her mate. Ignoring her own aches and injuries, she stumbled toward the edge of the concrete slab.

"Zac, where are you?" she called, petrified by the eerie silence that had fallen over the night. Even the occasional flashes of sunlight had ended.

Before she could panic and stagger down the residential lane to find him, her jaguar limped into view and became a battered man, covered in small bruises and minor scrapes.

Even though she could see he was fine with her eyes, it didn't stop River from feeling with her hands, touching every scrape and bruise until she was satisfied he was real, living, and breathing in front of her. "Are you all right?"

"Nothing's suffered except my pride." Zac groaned and popped his shoulder back into place. "Is it over?"

"Not quite. Lucia escaped." Through a freaking flaming door to some kind of unknown hellscape. The sulfurous scent of brimstone lingered in the air long after it was gone.

"Darrell?"

They both turned their gazes toward the motionless figure on the ground.

"I'm sor—"

"No." Zac shook his head and cupped her cheek. "Don't be sorry. He did this to himself. It went down the only way it could have."

"As for Lucia... I'm going to set all of the circle's resources into finding her."

"How are you going to convince them to do that?"

"I'm not asking. I'm going to *tell* them to do it. They wanted a goddess, well, now they're going to get one."

River briskly stepped away and crouched beside Rhona. Her chest rose and fell in shallow breaths. One by one, she examined the others and concluded only Grace had died. No matter what she thought of the stubborn old witch's policy toward male witches, her loss had been one death too many.

"They're all hurt. We'll need the others to help me carry them to safety."

"When Lucia gave me the slip, I crossed paths with Tommy while trying to hunt her down. They'll be here soon."

Setting her mouth into a determined line, River moved toward the foundation where Darrell's body lay. Magic had scarred and weathered the once-smooth concrete bed, leaving branching scorch marks and deep crevices behind.

True to Zac's word, Tommy limped around the corner with Maiara and Lyle a few steps behind him. All three looked battered, but River didn't spot any serious injuries. The alpha wolf stepped over and looked down at Darrell, features stormy despite his silence.

"The last few vampires bolted," Lyle told them. "We lost a wolf in the fight, and Harrison won't be flying for a couple weeks. They weren't much of anything but a cloud of mosquitoes to be honest. Ian's helping the wounded to safety."

"Are you three still able to fight?" River asked.

"We are," Maiara replied. "Where do we go next?"

River trained her gaze on the western horizon. "Now we go to Rosenhaven."

CHAPTER 18

At River's suggestion, Argus remained behind with a few of his wolves to take care of the injured shifters and comatose witches. Haverton and Morales vowed to respectfully remove Grace's body.

Meanwhile, Ian and Harrison drove the remaining able-bodied fighters to Rosenhaven. Despite his broken arm, the raven refused to be left behind, and he was also too stubborn to let anyone else drive his truck, claiming he didn't need both hands to haul a bunch of wolves around for a vampire hunt.

"So, I have some news for you," Ian said, "about your friend, Bobby, and you're not going to like it."

Zac leaned forward in his seat. "What is it?"

"Is he okay?" Tommy asked from the back.

"He's fine. Avery called before you all loaded into my vehicle, and she thought you might wanna know that Bobby remembered something about the night he was turned."

"Did he remember who turned him?"

"Oh yeah. And it's not a who. It's a them."

River snapped her gaze over. Then her belly sank with the creeping dread of realizing she'd been right all along despite her urgent desire to be wrong. "Who?"

Ian took another turn. He knew the way without needing directions from her. "Avery's pretty good at unraveling vampire charms, and she was able to make some progress with him tonight. Based on the description he gave, they're pretty damn certain it was those two knights who've been 'investigating' the issue." He raised one hand from the wheel and made air quotes. "Not too many red-headed twins around these parts, and he was adamant about it being a man and a woman with red hair."

Tommy and Zac both let loose a string of swears.

"I *knew* there was something up with those two," she said. "They didn't even try to look legit about their motives. What can we do? Anything?"

"Us? Nothing more than what we're going to do," Ian said as he turned onto the private road leading to the coven. "My acquaintance already phoned the vampire Council of Elders a few days back when she took Bobby for us. Hopefully they return her message soon and give enough of a damn about what's happening here."

"Well, I'm sick of waiting," River said. "I want answers tonight for all of the vampires that were there. They were… crazed. Like mindless animals more than anything else. I've never seen vampires like that before."

Lyle stroked his unshaven chin and slouched back in the seat. "Is it possible they were under a spell? I mean, like, something bad was done to all the juice from the bloody sacrament thing or whatever. What if the blood was tainted?"

River stiffened. "And they've turned newborn vampires into blood slaves."

The hound nodded. "Yeah. I mean, there's this one thing in common between all assholes like them, you get idiot lackeys to do the heavy lifting for you. I ought to know since I used to be one. Only difference is, my boss used to control me with drugs instead of blood."

"Same difference to a vampire," Ian said.

"Agreed. So what do we do? If they're vampire junkies with no choice in the matter, is there a way to spare them?"

"Doubtful," Ian said as he navigated onto another dark road, headlights set to high beam, "but River would know best. The way I understand it, the more potent the blood, the longer it remains in the vampire."

River clutched the armrest tight as the enormous plantation house came into view, each window glowing against the night. "That's right, and if they're using the tainted blood from the dark ritual, there's not much I can do on short notice. Grace was our expert on neutralizing the darkness. I've never trained in it. Never read up on it. Never *needed* to."

"And she's dead," Tommy muttered. "Just great."

Lyle growled low, the rumbling noise reverberating through his chest. "Then we'll have to put them out of their misery."

"Gate's open," Ian said as they reached the intimidating iron perimeter circling around a hundred acres of vampire territory. In the daylight it had been beautiful, the setting sun casting a golden glow over a green hill topped with the three-story home. Nighttime lent the property a cold and sinister appearance full of shadows.

Remaining on edge, River leaned forward in her seat. "I'll go up and ask for Margot while the rest of you wait here." Zacarias shot her a warning look, and rather than argue, she gave him a fragile smile. "Zac and I will go up. The rest of you hang here and keep those potions on hand."

"Solid plan," Ian said. "I had considered establishing a perimeter, but in the case of vampires, it's best to condense our numbers to one area. These little grenades of sunlight pack a damned fine punch. We don't want to be spread thin over the area for them to pick us off, if push comes to shove."

"After the shit they've put this town through, they have more than a few shoves coming at 'em, old man," Lyle replied.

Ian parked the car at the end of the drive beside the bubbling fountain. He exited the vehicle and waited with his water gun in hand, radiating the kind of confidence River had always wanted and never thought she could attain. "I'll be here if you need me."

Further down the impressive drive, Harrison lurked in his pickup truck with the members of Tommy's pack. When Ian barked a few orders to them, the massive shifters jumped down onto the concrete and began to take their defensive positions.

Her fellow witches may not have been able to stand beside her, but she had the aid of everyone else who mattered. With Zacarias at her side, the silent support she needed, River stalked up the long path to the steps and rapped against the door.

Everything about the atmosphere had changed, the air no longer lively with vampire activity, but cold and quiet. When they'd left Rosenhaven after sunset before, there had been vampires on the porch, and lively conversation echoing throughout.

Stone-cold silence emanated from within the antique manor, tracing cold fingers of terror up and down her spine. Goose bumps arose across her flesh and an unforgiving iron band closed around her ribs.

Breathe, River. Breathe, she told herself before raising the door knocker. It thudded heavily against the wood, and the longest, most excruciating twenty-three seconds of her life passed. The blood thundered in her head. She licked her dry lips and put on a brave face when the door opened to reveal a pale, brunette vampiress with glittering green eyes.

"May I help you?" she asked.

"We want to speak to Tremaine," River replied.

"Master Tremaine is currently indisposed."

Something wild and frenzied came over River, and before she knew what she was doing, she barged inside uninvited and poked her finger into the woman's chest. Something sizzled against her skin and singed the hairs on her arms. While it was probably an ancient ward established by another witch in trade, River burst through it like tearing a ribbon of tissue paper. "Well, you better find his ass because I'm about to rain fire on this plantation, starting with *you*. Don't think I can do it? Ask the dozen vampires who met me at Club Delirium. Oh, wait, guess you can't. They're ashes now."

The blood and color drained from the woman's face. "I'll get him."

"I'm already here, Samantha. It's all right. Go assist Lady Calloway with the remainder of the preparations, will you?"

Samantha inclined her head and hurried by, while Tremaine moved closer.

"Less than half an hour ago, my town was overrun by vampires, your fledglings, or whatever you want to call them. The funny thing is, some of them still had identification and driver's licenses on them, and when our police chief ran them, he found almost all those folks were reported missing within the past month."

"I have nothing to do with that. We have strict rules related to the creation of vampiric progeny, and if some rogue drifter created a crisis—"

"It wasn't a drifter! Even if it was, the responsibility still falls to your coven to handle the situation," River said tersely. "The countless vampires we've killed tonight surpasses a reasonable amount."

"You cannot come in here making baseless accusations."

"I can," River bluffed. "We've already figured out what's going on. When that warlock committed his Blood Sacrament, the bounty went to this coven, didn't it? You or Margot, or some other vampire here, used a bunch of neophytes to try to take out the shifter leaders in town. I may not be able to get the evidence from their ash piles, but I bet if we search this plantation, we'll find what we need. Won't we?"

Tremaine's smile never faltered, etched across his handsome face in stone. "We're done here."

"No, we're n—"

The report of a handgun echoed across the night sky, and then a shotgun boomed. River spun around with her hands raised in a protective gesture, summoning energy from her bangles to create a shield.

When she glanced around toward Tremaine again, there was nothing to see but open doorway and an empty foyer.

"Fucker bolted." Zac tensed and took a single step forward, but River grabbed his arm and pulled him back.

"Forget Tremaine. Don't go in there."

"Why not?"

Everything in her screamed not to go inside, recognizing the trap awaiting them in the unfamiliar corridors teeming with vampiric life. She couldn't pin the sensation, but there was something ancient and powerful tainting the manor's depths.

In the split seconds they were distracted with Tremaine, the vampires had closed the net around them. River and Zac hurried down the porch steps, only for Ian's voice to call out a warning to get down. The vet had crouched beside his vehicle, using it as a shield as he shot streams of concentrated sunlight into the darkness. A wolf howled, inhuman cries filled the air, and battle spilled onto the green lawn.

The vampires had come armed with martial weapons and firearms.

"Watch out! I think they have silver!" River called toward the group. Before they could reach their friends, another shot rang out and clipped her defensive shield. Gunfire lit the night, and then a flash erupted from a shattered vial. It reduced the vampires surrounding Ian into flaming silhouettes and crumbling dust, buying them time to race toward Ian. Blood seeped from a hole in the eagle shifter's shoulder. The moment she touched it to apply pressure, he grunted and swatted her hand away.

"I heal faster than most shifters. Special gift. I'll be fine. You worry about the ones shooting at us."

One by one, the lights on the property dimmed until there wasn't a single bulb burning inside or outside the house.

"Did you set the plantation on fire?" Ian asked.

"What?" River jerked her attention toward the house. Smoke wafted toward the sky and flames danced beyond a few open windows. "No. We didn't do anything but talk."

"Classic tactic for covering up their tracks."

Glowing eyes pierced the darkness from the edges of the roof and across the green pasture, pinpricks of red against the midnight canvas.

"Did you think we didn't expect your arrival?" a loud voice boomed toward them.

River whirled with her hands raised, crackling energy dancing between two identical force bracelets on her wrists. Rosenhaven's master of combat faced them from the eastern lawn. There was no way he could be anyone else when he was armed to the teeth like an action hero ready to smoke and punch his way through a ninety-minute summer blockbuster. While he wasn't an enormous man, size could be deceptive when it came to their kind. Muscle had nothing to do with a vampire's physical strength. Blood gleamed against his ivory fangs and smoke arose from his skin where golden beams from puddles of liquid sunlight shone over him. Blisters rippled over his skin, not that he seemed to notice or care.

Until now, River hadn't known any vampire could withstand the sunlight. Not for more than a few seconds, and certainly not for any sustained amount of time. He stepped forward out of the path of the sunbeam. Within moments, the damage healed.

"You were foolish to come here tonight. We are unstoppable now that Margot has given us a true gift." The vampire's eyes gleamed reddish gold in the dim light. "Attack!"

More frenzied vampires and thralls rushed out from the tree line bordering the property. Most had the look of the homeless about them, but others wore suits and summer dresses. The sheer number took River by surprise, and she wondered how many cities they had taken people from to go unnoticed.

Tommy raced across the grass and crashed into the combat master. They tumbled across the ground and came up with fangs bared. The alpha's gigantic size didn't seem to give him any advantage against the abnormally strong vampire. One punch from him launched Tommy several yards away where he tumbled over the grass. Then the vampire was up again, shotgun in his hands as the remaining wolves charged. The next wolf rushed into a blast, yelped, and fell motionless on the ground.

Ian swore and tensed as if he were going to rush out toward the fallen alpha. "There's too many of them."

Four vampires clung to Maiara's shaggy back while another two alternated rushing Lyle. Everywhere River looked, her friends were being overrun. Harrison kept up a steady stream from his water gun, but the reservoir was running low. Ian lobbed the last of his sunlight vials, but his target blurred across the ground, no longer there when the potion landed. Even with two wolves hanging off him, desperately attempting to rip him limb from limb, the master of combat seemed unstoppable.

I have to stop this. I have to end it now.

River stepped out from behind the armored car.

"River?" Zac's alarmed voice reached her before he grabbed her wrist. "You can't go out there."

"Stay here," she murmured, pulling her hand away from him effortlessly, as if his grip had barely been there.

A spark ignited in her left hand, small and insignificant at first, but she fed it with her anger, fear, and her desire to protect her friends. She cast aside her doubts and dug down deep within herself, drawing on a confidence she hadn't realized was there. The spark pulsed, doubling in size as it drew on her strength, but it still wasn't enough.

I won't let them hurt anyone else, she told herself. *I won't be afraid.*

The world around River erupted in golden light. It spread in a magnificent wave across hundreds of feet, flooding down the property and washing over every building. With nowhere to run or hide, vampires sizzled and combusted into piles of ash.

Her head throbbed a warning for her to stop, and a buzz filled her ears. Too tenacious to succumb to the pain, she clung to consciousness and the spell as exhaustion fluttered at the edge of her thoughts.

She had to hold it, had to sear the resplendence of her spell into their collective memory until every vampire from Texas to the great covens across the ocean shared their pain.

She moved across the front lawn with light blazing from her fingertips, her arms, and every inch of her body uncovered by clothing. She'd become the sun itself, radiant and emanating raw power. Several vampires rushed at her without care for the danger, too crazed to stop. They were incinerated on the spot, exploding into ash and cinders before they came within five yards of River. Those with their minds intact fled, but not all of them were fast enough.

With Zac alongside him, Tommy pounced the master of combat to the ground and pinned him there. They mauled him mercilessly while he shrieked and writhed until the vampire was nothing more than dust and bones.

With the final vestiges of strength she possessed, River pushed on the spell. It was as if a shockwave had gone off, an explosion with no sound. Sunlight rippled outward in a full circle and washed across the property.

***

When River stirred, she was no longer standing and Zac had enfolded her in his strong arms. He sat on the grass while holding her trembling body in his lap. Meanwhile, piles of smoldering ash surrounded them on the manicured lawn and an out of control fire raged through the ivory plantation house.

How long had she been out?

"Zac?"

"I got you." Zacarias squeezed her for emphasis. "Are you okay?"

"As okay as I can be after using so much magic." She felt cold all over, shivering like a diabetic friend she'd had in college when she'd gone into insulin shock. "Was I out for long?"

"Not even twenty minutes. Maiara and Tommy's pack are picking off the vamps that try to escape the house," he murmured against her ear. "Guess there were a few trapped inside. You seemed okay, so we didn't want to move you yet."

"Glad you waited... Don't want any survivors here. I just need a few more moments."

A few minutes more than circumstance wanted her to have, apparently. A black sedan rolled into the drive and came to a stop behind Ian's SUV. Everyone still on their feet tensed and readied themselves for more trouble. Ian gestured toward the werewolf on his right, and then the shifters fanned out.

River held up her hand against the beam of the headlights until they flicked off, leaving dazzling stars in her eyes. A low growl rumbled in Zac's chest, but he didn't move away from her.

"River Jackson?" a feminine voice called from the parked car.

"Help me up," she murmured to the agitated panther. Zac rose and brought her with him as the door opened and two figures emerged, both wearing sophisticated black suits tailored to their frames, although it must have taken a dozen yards of fabric to clothe the tall man. Both were dark skinned, like polished ebony with a muted silver sheen over flawless features and stoic faces. Their eyes shone amber, reflecting the flames raging over the plantation house.

Vampires.

"Are you River Jackson?" the woman asked again. She shut the passenger door and stepped forward.

River stepped in front of Zac and raised one hand, praying she had enough power left for two more. Either forewarned by the others, or possessing the sense her fellow vampires had lacked, the woman drew short of approaching.

"Hold there," she cried with both of her hands out. "We're not your enemy."

"You're a vampire, and after what we've experienced, you certainly look like one right now," Zacarias said.

"Allow me the chance to introduce myself. I am Overseer Heloise McKnight, and the tall, silent one is Champion Antonin Dragomir."

"What do you want?" River asked.

"Answers. Only answers. We were sent by Chancellor Julius to investigate charges against Lady Margot Calloway."

River blinked. "What charges?"

"Negligence and dereliction of her duties. Word has reached the Council of Elders regarding the recent events in Atropos, and Margot had not reported any of it. That in itself is a severe breach of protocol. Murder and so much witch activity requires immediate action and a prompt disclosure to the council. We came to take her into our custody."

"You all keep tabs on us?"

Heloise arched one delicate eyebrow. "Do you not do the same regarding our kind?"

"Fair point," River conceded.

"It seems you handled the problem for us," Antonin said. His voice rumbled, low and guttural but thick with a Russian accent. He gazed at the burning plantation house without pity or sadness.

"You're not upset?" Zac asked incredulously. His gaze darted from River to the vampires and back again.

"Why should we be?" Heloise asked.

"We didn't start the fire," River blurted.

"I did not say you had." Overseer Heloise crossed her slender arms against her chest. "As far as I'm concerned, you may very well have performed my duties *for* me."

"Wait, you mean you would have burned this place down just because they didn't report in?" Zac's brows drew together.

Heloise blinked. "You didn't realize?"

"Realize what?"

"There has been… an upheaval in Rosenhaven. A cold civil war of sorts. A single message for assistance reached the Council of Elders before all communications ceased. Between this and our reports from Lady Avery, we came as quickly as we were able."

"I thought there may be some disagreements, but I can't say we ran into anyone who looked like they opposed Margot and Tremaine. Everyone attacked us on sight, without provocation."

The Overseer pursed her lips. "No one?"

"No one," Zac repeated. "We stepped inside to talk to Tremaine and they attacked our friends outside."

"That's particularly unusual, as I have an e-mail sent from Mistress Felicity."

"She's dead," River said in a flat voice. "At least that's what we were told when we first approached the coven a week ago for assistance about the vampire attack in town. Tremaine had taken her place."

Heloise's features darkened, although her eyes still shone livid red. "Margot did *not* report Felicity's death to us. Did you destroy her?"

"I have no idea. We didn't see her, and Tremaine hauled ass."

"Damn." Heloise's lips twisted and she drummed her fingers against the side of her thigh.

Antonin cracked his knuckles. "I say we go drag them out."

"We can't very well go inside while it is still burning, Antonin. The fire will cleanse whoever remains," Heloise replied to her companion. She turned her back on the raging inferno and faced River. "Had we known things were so serious, we would have come at once. Felicity's e-mail implied interpersonal problems between her and Margot. The usual kind of power struggle that sometimes takes place. It wasn't until we received a call from Lady Avery that we knew something more was amiss. I would consider it a personal favor if you led me through the events we've missed."

With her adrenaline fast fading away, River's shoulders slumped, but she gestured to the back of Tommy's truck. If she was going to go over everything, she damn well wanted to sit down. Once she was settled, she cleared her throat and started from the very beginning.

"Right. So it all began the day we discovered a warlock was working with the vampires."

Epilogue

In the aftermath of the attack, River crawled into bed and slept for a full day, rousing for brief moments when Zac tried to awaken her for food. She had a single vague memory of shambling to the bathroom and then gobbling down a bowl of oatmeal before she passed back out again under the covers.

River honestly thought she could sleep for a week, but there was too much to do. Calls to make, witches to meet, and a total restructuring of everything they'd ever known about their society, especially since Darrell's scheme had magically incapacitated their most capable witches. By escaping with his trinket, Lucia had taken their powers with her. On top of that, they hadn't torn Darrell's magical essence from his spirit to prevent him from returning in another life. One day, he'd be back with all of the knowledge he'd learned in his most recent life intact.

Instead of making calls, she sat as useless as a bump on a log on her living room sofa while Maiara napped beside her. Zac and Harrison decided to work from home, and since his computer had been trashed, River allowed her fiancé to conduct business on her PC.

Chief Haverton called to let them know Joe had been cleared of all charges and released. The local news had a field day with the story of Darrell's brutal killing spree across Atropos, especially since he'd taken the lives of an old woman visiting a good friend and Officer Clark. Every recent loss of life was attributed to his crimes.

River dreaded the upcoming memorial service for all his victims, but her mother had promised to fly in and stand beside her in support. Between Zac and her mom, that was all she needed.

Maybe life would finally become normal again, even if there were a half-dozen Overseers arriving from across the United States to investigate Rosenhaven's fall. Heloise had provided advanced warning, promising they would keep to themselves.

Before River could nod off and fall asleep with Maiara, the phone rang. She plucked it up before her snoozing bear friend could awaken and moved from the living room.

"Hello?"

"Hello, River," Heloise greeted her.

"Hi. How's it going? Any news?"

"Plenty. A few escapee neophytes told us everything we needed to know before we were forced to put them down. It seems Margot fed a kind of... powerful blood to them in the days before the attacks. A blood infused with magic."

"The blood from the ritual Darrell performed," River breathed, gleaning sudden understanding about the vampires' rabid behavior. "Lyle was right. Our friend theorized that may be the case with the blood."

"Yes. It was how she controlled them all."

"Do you think it's how that one big guy withstood our sunlight bombs?"

"Not exactly," Heloise answered after a brief pause. "I believe something more insidious was at work, and after some consideration, I've decided to share our findings with you."

"Okay. What did you find?"

"It isn't common knowledge outside of our society, but one of our Ancients slept beneath Rosenhaven in a protected chamber. It was barely affected by the fire, but what I discovered disturbed me most of all. Margot and the masters appear to have drained Lamashtu, our ancestor. That is why they survived the potions, and that is why it is imperative we find Margot."

Air whistled over River's teeth as she sucked in a sharp breath. "I'm guessing that's really, really bad."

"To put it lightly, yes. Along with Lamashtu's remains, we found a set of brittle bones in a suit on the outskirts of the property, and the style matches your description of Tremaine."

"Good riddance. I guess Margot didn't want to share any more of the power with him."

"So it would seem," Heloise said. "There is no crime in our society worse than the cannibalization of another vampire. Margot may have possibly drained two."

"What about the creepy twin knights who turned our friend?"

"Ah, yes. Your friend. Rest assured, none of this has tainted him. He's become quite wealthy, in fact, as the

Council of Elders has chosen to pay reparations to him for his suffering. As for the Carmichaels, they remain unaccounted for at this time." Irritation seeped into her voice, a low and husky growl of displeasure. "I find it difficult to believe they would be involved in such dirty business, but the fact that they've gone into hiding doesn't speak well for them."

They spoke a few more minutes before River hung up, apprehension numbing her fingers and toes as she considered the danger brewing around them. It was bad enough knowing Lucia was out there somewhere, and now there was a supercharged vampire as well.

Sighing, River returned to the living room and settled down to enjoy the final day with her new friends. Lyle sometimes sprawled across the floor to watch television with the her and Maiara, true to his canine nature, while Ian spent his downtime catching up with Argus. He claimed he didn't want to bore the kids with his old fuddy-duddy ways.

She figured Ian's long career as a military officer wouldn't allow him to sit still and twiddle his thumbs, so he was handling work where it wouldn't bother the rest of them. She also figured she should follow his example, but she couldn't muster up the drive. Not yet, at least. The most she had done was call in to check on Pythia's condition.

Due to the extent of Pythia's injuries, several witches had put their talents together and brewed a bevy of restorative potions to get their fellow witch back on her feet.

Of course, it may have helped that River had no qualms about exposing Pythia's true identity as the Mother and spread the news to anyone who would listen. What was the point of having leaders if they shrouded themselves behind a pompous mystery to prohibit anyone asking for help? Hiding from the normal humans was one thing, but all the internal secrets were more of a hindrance than an asset.

Beginning with Georgina then working her way down the line of licensed alchemists, she told anyone who would listen. One of their sisters in Austin, also a registered nurse, agreed to take a week's vacation from work to nurture Pythia's recovery until her bones mended. In a week, the doctors would be releasing her from the hospital, and River hadn't decided whether she wanted to be there or not.

Would her presence be welcomed at all? Reconciling with Pythia was yet another thing to add to her long list of issues to handle. Including Grace's funeral. The date had been set for the upcoming weekend.

So many funerals.

"Car's loaded," Ian called out, yanking River from her thoughts.

Beside her, Maiara roused from her doze and blinked up at the eagle shifter. "Time to go?"

"If you're ready," Ian said. "If we leave now, we can be home before nightfall."

"I am prepared," the bear replied.

"Me too." Lyle popped in from the kitchen with a bucket of leftover fried chicken in hand. "You mind if we take this with us?"

Zac grinned. "Go ahead."

"Thanks for all your help, Lyle. You too, Ian." River hugged each man in turn. "We wouldn't have managed this without you."

"Ah, think nothin' of it," Lyle said. His bashful smile preceded a tip of his head. "Glad to have helped. You let us know if you need us back down here to track that leech."

"I think the vampires have that covered," River said.

Lyle's amiable smile never faded. "Still, keep us updated. If you ever need anything, we're only a few hours away."

"Don't be surprised if I ever call you to help up in Quickdraw," Ian added, grinning. "We get our own share of problems from time to time, and a witch would certainly be a help to us."

"Anytime you need me, I'll be there," River promised. "What's next for you two?"

Lyle's brown eyes lit up with unconcealed longing. "Family time. I miss the pups."

"You mean your three little hellions," Ian joked, patting Lyle on the shoulder in sympathy. "You'd have to pay me to babysit those kids again."

Chuckling and bickering at each other in the way only a father and son could do, the two men meandered down the drive toward Ian's SUV. Lyle waved before he climbed into the passenger side, and then they waited for the bear shifter to say her goodbyes. Maiara couldn't drive legally— though she'd done a stellar job apparently while bringing River back to Atropos after the attack at the Delirium.

"What about you, Maiara? Still going back to the forests?"

"After I speak with the human den, yes, for a time I believe I will roam and enjoy what remains of this summer."

"Well, you're always welcome to come back here and visit. Who knows, after all this, I may give in and let Zac have a pool and jacuzzi installed."

A broad grin spread over Maiara's face. Her tight hug realigned River's spine and popped it noisily. "I would like that, and to spend more time with your never-ending library of books with shirtless covers."

River laughed and rubbed her back. "Not a problem."

The three shifters left together. River closed the door and stood in the entry a few moments, taken aback by the silence. After so many days of people and noise, the emptiness struck her as foreign and strange. For all the time she'd wanted her peace and privacy back, she'd finally received it and no longer wanted it.

"You okay?" Zac asked.

"Yeah. Tired, I guess."

"Well, if anyone deserves a rest, it's you." He extended his hand. When she took it, he tugged her into the living room. No sign of her fight with Darrell remained, unless she counted the new furniture and monstrously large television that had been delivered earlier that morning.

"What's really bugging you?" Zac asked as he dropped to the couch and pulled her down into his lap.

"I don't know what to do with myself now that it's over." She gazed out the window, disinterested in the superhero flick playing on the television.

"I can think of a few things." He waggled his brows and pinched her bottom.

"You know what I mean." She swatted his hand and wiggled against his lap.

"Nothing has to change. You're still you, no matter who you might have been once upon a time in some myth far, far away."

"You really mangled that one. No wonder the team won't allow you to help with the dialogue writing."

"Hey. I do my best."

Their shared laughter was a much needed relief after everything they had gone through. His words, genuine despite the teasing delivery, lifted some of the weight from her shoulders.

"I guess what really worries me is that you'll see me differently somehow," she confessed.

"Nah," Zac said as he kissed the top of her head. "You were always a goddess to me. The only difference is, now everyone else is going to know it too."

ABOUT THE AUTHOR

Vivienne Savage is a resident of a small town in rural Texas. While she isn't concocting sexy ways for shapeshifters and humans to find their match, she raises two children and works as a nurse in a rural retirement home.